Never

Give

Up

Renee Jean

Never Give Up is dedicated to my mom Gail Gage Fournier. Thank you for always believing in me and allowing me to chase my dreams no matter where they take me.

Chapter 1

"...5,6,7,8. Come on ladies, keep your posture, follow the music and for the love of God, smile! Can we please just try to be together one time?" Sabrina stomped her foot as she watched the dancers move. "Alright now, piquet, lift, get ready, wait, and now, kick. Kick! And again. First group go, second group now, third and fourth. Ok now relevé, hold it, strong arms. Feel it burn, that's right, hold your poses until the music is done." Sabrina Marks, head choreographer and owner of the Marks Performance Company sighed. "Alright people, well that didn't suck completely, I guess. We're done for the day, go home. I'm sick of looking at you."

The exhausted dancers swept toward the dressing area to gather their collective belongings while Sabrina took to the floor to begin marking out a combination. With hesitant glances back the group trudged on. One by one they made their way out the door. One of the last performers was Akaylia Jean Reynolds. Wide-eyed and fresh to the program she often lingered after rehearsal, just taking in the atmosphere. Lost in her own world staring up into the balcony she jumped when a voice invaded her daydreams.

"Kaylie!" She spun around quickly, nearly tripping over her own feet. Standing before her was Sabrina, stretching. Kaylie hated when she did that. Her body seemed to be made of rubber; she didn't need to stretch. Regaining her balance, she attempted to look her boss in the eye.

"Yes?" she squeaked. Clearing her throat she straightened then tried again. "Yes Sabrina?"

"You're still here, I see."

"Sorry, I didn't mean to bother you. I'll get out of your way."
She headed for the door willing the heat rising in her cheeks to go
away.

"Get back here." Akaylia froze, terrified. Fearing she more than
offended the iconic choreographer, she shrunk into the shadows,
slowly turning around. Sabrina was center stage, watching her. She
couldn't help but wonder what she'd done wrong. Taking a deep
breath she emerged back onto the stage inching toward her mentor.

"Stop looking like a dog about to get beat," she snapped. "I
wanted to tell you I thought you looked good in rehearsal."

Kaylie straightened up trying to comprehend what she just heard.
Sabrina never complimented anyone; her ears must be playing
tricks on her. The stress was obviously getting to her. She
continued standing there; hoping the awkward moment would
pass. She'd never even talked to Sabrina one on one since the day
she joined the company, now here she was stuck, waiting for the
other shoe to drop. Taking a deep breath she made her way to
center stage and the idol she so desperately wanted to impress.
Gathering everything she could muster she looked up managing to
squeak out "Is there something I can do for you Sabrina?"

Sabrina crossed her arms, watching the young dancer squirm.
"Yes, as a matter of fact. You're going to do a combination for me,
assuming you are up for it." With that she spun and stalked toward
the soundboard without waiting for confirmation. Glancing back
she smirked at the lack of belief on Kaylie's face. She turned back
to the switches in front of her. "Don't just stand there, get ready.
I'm going to play the music then show what I want you to do, got
it?"

She really didn't, but Kaylie tried to look prepared as she waited
for the beat to start. She began wringing her hands as thoughts
shoved one another, vying for space in her brain. Why had Sabrina
chosen her? Dozens of other dancers were much stronger not to
mention had significant seniority over her, why would Sabrina

want to have her be the one showing this combination. What sort of sadistic game was she playing? Kaylie attempted to shake off the nerves now creeping up her spine. She focused, listening intently to the music as it drifted hauntingly from the speakers. The music was instrumental with a melancholy after tone and the emotion wrapped within it was powerful even for the few bars that played. It told a story without a cast of characters yet there was story nonetheless. She could feel it, loss but yet a sense of continuing on at the same time. She closed her eyes allowing each note to float through her leaving an invisible but very real impression upon her soul. It was the most beautiful piece she had heard since she began dancing. Just as quickly as it started, it was cut off. Sabrina materialized in front of her once again, startling her back to reality.

Without a word she began to move, painting a picture with the contortions and flow of her body. Kaylie felt she could hear the music through the movements even without a note being played. That profound sorrow and passionate optimism she felt course through her veins when the sound was on now played out through every extension and contraction. Every turn Sabrina made brought up another dimension of this amazing piece. When she melted at the end Kaylie had to quickly wipe away a tear.

Sabrina twisted to face her making Kaylie shrink under the intense stare as she tried fruitlessly to hide her fear. She knew the choreographer would see through her like a piece of glass but still she tried. Squaring her shoulders she lifted her chin. She took a deep breath then opened her mouth to comment but Sabrina cut her off. "Stand right here," she snapped pointing directly next to her. "Hurry up. Don't make me wait."

Kaylie quickly strode to where she had been summoned, taking the pose she observed at the beginning of the combination. Sabrina counted out the movements going back over each eight count a second time as she added on. Kaylie was a quick learner but she could feel the cold fingers of terror creeping up, causing her to struggle. Pushing the panic down she forced all her concentration on the dance, doing her best to pick up each and every step.

Hitting the last pose she froze like a statue and, and waited for the next instruction. "Practice that a few times and get it down then I want to see it with the music, understand?" With that she disappeared into the shadows without waiting for a response. Kaylie watched her go, wondering what crazed mind game she was playing now. She walked back to center stage and took the original position. For one terrifying moment she drew a blank forgetting every precious count of the combination. Closing her eyes she listened to the music in her mind. Felt the incredible emotion sweeping over her once again and it all came flooding back.

Her body moved on its own, tracing the lines Sabrina had created and she let herself be taken to a distant place. Every second was a moment of bliss and sadness swirling together as she danced across the stage. She struck the final move, held it for almost a full minute catching her breath before she began to move again. Transitioning into the beginning pose she started the combination all over. Each count taking her further into the imaginary world that was created in the heart of anyone the music touched. She heard it play in her mind yet was surrounded by the silence that enveloped the auditorium.

She finished again and just as she gathered her strength to practice one more time, Sabrina appeared at the edge of her vision. She always did that. Waiting until someone was almost comfortable with a combination she would put them on the spot; making them perform then point out every mistake. Trembling internally, Kaylie forced a smile and held her stance.

"Take your pose Ms. Reynolds, I want to see you perform this." She didn't turn around as she sauntered to the soundboard. Kaylie still stood frozen in place watching her instructor. "I said take your position, it's time to do this thing."

"Yes Sabrina, sorry Sabrina." Kaylie scurried across the stage and took the beginning pose. She closed her eyes waiting for the music to transport her. Holding her position and her breath she anticipated the start. It was taking forever and she could feel the muscles in her legs and arms starting to tremble. Just as she felt she was going to collapse, the music began. Holding the first couple bars, she surrendered her body to the movements that the music required.

Passion overtaking her, she twisted and leapt. Each note coursing through her veins, taking her to their enchanted world, she moved. She felt as though she was floating; simply being moved by the current of the music. She danced with all the power and emotion she possessed, each and every second passing without notice.

All too soon the combination ended and the music was cut off. Kaylie melted to the ending pose then ultimately to the floor, gasping for breath. She felt as though her entire body had been crying and recovering again and again. Her breathing eased after a moment. She got to her unsteady feet turning to face Sabrina. Steeling herself for the oncoming criticism, she raised her gaze and locked eyes with the poker-faced choreographer.

Sabrina just stood there in the shadows watching her, no satisfaction or unhappiness on her face. She was motionless and emotionless. After what felt like an eternity, she finally moved into the light and approached the terrified dancer. She had the tiniest of smirks as she observed the terrified girl in front of her. But it wasn't until she was just a few feet away that Kaylie could see the crack in stone; Sabrina had tears in her eyes.

Immediately uneasy, Kaylie ran through the routine in her head. Had she forgotten a step? Missed the starting time? Gotten off the beat somehow? She couldn't figure it out, but clearly she had done something very wrong. She felt sick and on the verge of tears herself. How could she have screwed up such an incredible performance? Why did she disgrace the most powerful piece of music she had ever heard?

Kaylie could feel her heart sinking, as her own tears were about to spill over when Sabrina broke the silence. Kaylie flinched at the sound of her voice not even hearing the words the first time through. She peeked up, saw Sabrina's smile, and was instantly confused.

"What?" she managed to get out.

"I said I knew I picked the right person to perform that."

"I did ok?" The world was spinning. How could this be coming from the same person that tore dancers apart as a form of mild amusement?

"You did better than ok. I wanted to see this performed with passion and emotion. I knew you would be the perfect person to do it."

"What is it for?" she immediately regretted asking. It was obviously going to be something for the new summer recital. Everything they worked on recently was for that concert. It would be a dream to perform it but she was way to green to be chosen. However the flicker of hope remained, after all she was the one that got to try it out first.

"For the new summer show Kaylie. Thinking about having it as the opening number. This would be the beginning part and I am thinking a solo."

"A solo?"

"Yeah, then have the rest of the cast join in and build up the number."

"Sounds good," she couldn't stop herself. "Who were you thinking for the solo?"

Sabrina took another step toward her bringing them within inches of each other and as she leaned in Kaylie could feel herself tightening up nearly standing at attention. "I was sort of thinking that you could do it."

The world went sideways as Kaylie lost the feeling in her legs. She hit the stage hard but recovered as quickly as she could. Embarrassed, she got back to her feet in a hurry. "Are you sure?"

"Yes I'm sure," Sabrina whispered still leaning in.

"I never thought that I..." Kaylie trailed off her breath caught in her throat.

"I know you didn't but it will work just fine." She spun and stalked off. Then almost as an after thought she called back over her shoulder, "just don't mess this up."

Kaylie stayed frozen in place watching the receding silhouette. That actually just happened. She really just got a solo. She had only been with the company 6 months. Staggering toward the door she absentmindedly grabbed her bag, wandering right past the dressing room. She was just about to head outside into the blistering cold of Chicago's winter when one of the building security guards snatched her by the arm.

"Miss it's winter out there, where's your coat?" Startled from her thoughts she tripped back and slipped onto a chair against the wall. He came forward to help her but she held up her hand to let him know she was all right.

"Sorry, I got it." She stood back up straightening her clothes. Once she was satisfied that the awkwardness of the moment had passed she walked back down to the dressing area, changed into her street clothes, and bundled up. Getting back to the door she stopped.

"Thanks Arthur, guess I was in my own world there."

"No problem, Miss." He was always so polite. Arthur was an elderly man. He always held the door and tipped his hat for the misses and gave a slight bow of his head for the sirs. "Well, have a good night."

"You too, see you Monday." Taking a step out into the wind she stood for a moment letting the moment sink the rest of the way in.

Once she felt the light-headedness of excitement dwindle down enough she started heading for the L.

It was freezing outside and the wind, which the city is so famous for, cut through her clothes straight to the bone. She barely noticed. A few blocks from the auditorium she got to the station and climbed the stairs up to the platform.

The train was packed. People were crowding the seats, bumping into each other as they jostled for room and places to hold onto the railings. Kaylie put in her headphones turning on her mp3 player to drown out the subway noise. She glanced down at her hands; they were shaking. Life was going so well right now she couldn't imagine it getting any better. Now all she wanted to do was get home and tell Garrett all about her exciting news.

She knew she could just call him but he would just be getting home from work and with all the noise on the L this time of day he would struggle to hear her. She would also never be able to make out what his tired voice was saying.

The train swayed and she clutched the handrail a little tighter to keep from being knocked off her feet. There was a tiny metallic *clink* when she squeezed the rail. She glanced down at her ring that had caused it. Staring back at her was the modest diamond ring Garrett had surprised her with just over one year ago. It may not be the biggest diamond or the shiniest gold but to her it was immaculate and priceless.

She lifted her finger and smiled as the harsh fluorescent lights gleamed against the stone. She was so caught up she nearly missed the fact her stop was next. Not the longest trip, but she was glad to get the chance to ride the train instead of the cost of a cab. She slid around the couple next to her pressing her way toward the door. Scanning the platform for her path through the crowd she shifted her dance bag to her other shoulder as she waited for the door to open.

The robotic voice overhead told her the train had reached her stop and to please make room for those exiting the train once the doors had opened. With barely more than a foot of space she shoved past the doors and sprinted for the stairs leading to the street. Taking them two at a time she quickly descended. She then made a right, heading back behind the stairway down the street in one fluid movement. She was in great shape but already out of breath. She wasn't focused on her breathing while she ran, just on getting home.

Garrett was going to be so excited to hear her news. She just wanted to get to him and shout from the rooftops how great her day had been. People milling about on the sidewalk blocked her path. She struggled to get past them. It felt like she was moving in slow motion no matter how fast she went. Finally she jumped off the curb running instead along the bike path on the side of the road. She knew that commuters were probably looking at her like she was crazy but she didn't care.

She turned onto her street pushing her legs to go even faster as her building came into view just a couple blocks ahead. Her mid-rise apartment building looked just like every other building on the street but to her it was a golden temple awaiting her arrival. And inside she would find her prince.

She breezed into the lobby, past the elevators, heading straight up the stairs. She just couldn't stand still in that metal box waiting for it to reach her floor. She paused for just a moment on the fourth floor landing to catch her breath not wanting to be gasping when she made her announcement. Standing and adjusting her bag that had miraculously stayed on her shoulder during the mini marathon she put it through, she forced her legs to walk up the last two flights of stairs then calmly down the hall. Fishing for her keys she approached the door.

Just as she found her apartment key on the ring the door swung open. Before she could react she was enveloped in a huge bear hug. For just a minute she forgot about her big news and just breathed him in. Garrett was six foot two inches tall and one hundred eighty pounds. His body framed hers' in a warm, comforting embrace that shut out the rest of the world. He pulled back as he leaned down kissing her cheek then gave a quick peck to her lips.

Standing there beaming that amazing smile she had fallen in love with the first time she saw it, she couldn't help but wonder if she could make it any brighter. She dropped her bag on the little table by the door like she always did setting her mp3 player next to it with the music still blaring from the headphones.

She opened her mouth to make her announcement when he cut her off. "I know I'm not supposed to know, but congratulations baby!" He was practically shouting as he hugged her again. "You deserve this so much. I am so proud of you."

She was completely shocked. Kaylie stepped back, looking at him quizzically. She wasn't sure if he actually knew or if he was congratulating her for something else. Finally she asked him, "What are you talking about?"

"You got the solo in the summer concert, didn't you?"

"Yeah, but how did you know?"

"My firm got the advertising account for the dance company and they gave us a lot of information for the posters and flyers, one piece was that there was going to be a solo and your name was listed as the performer."

"Oh. Well I wanted to tell you but," she hugged him and started jumping up and down. "I'm just so excited!"

"I think we should go celebrate tonight, dinner at Café Le Amile."

"Really? That place is so expensive. And are you sure it's worth going out over just getting a solo?"

"Just a solo? Baby, you are amazing. You deserve to go out and celebrate all the time. You deserve everything your heart desires so go get changed and we will have a wonderful night."

She was speechless as she stood there staring at him. He looked back at her smiling then turned to go get ready. She skipped off down the hall after him stripping off her sweaty clothing. Dropping them in a pile on the bathroom floor she turned the shower on and let down her ponytail while the water was heating up. She smiled in the gathering steam; life was perfect.

Showering had never been a time consuming ordeal for Kaylie and she made short work of it tonight. Rinsing the shampoo then conditioner through her hair she mentally roamed her closet figuring out what she wanted to wear. There were so many options from dresses to suits and of course casual but there was no way she was putting on a pair of jeans to go to Café Le Amile. The suits were beautiful and tailored. She knew she looked good in them but tonight was a romantic night. It called for her favorite little black dress.

She jumped out of the shower toweling her wet hair until it stopped dripping. She should have been cold after emerging from the steamy shower into the drafty apartment but her excitement kept her warm while she hurriedly located the dress and her black heels to go with it. Slipping into the body hugging black dress she adjusted the strapless top and carried her shoes back to the bathroom to finish getting ready.

Her hair looked nice up but she had been a dancer her entire life so wearing it up was also part of the job. For special occasions she liked to mix it up and wear it down. However this presented a challenge as she had naturally wavy hair. It would take twenty minutes to blow dry it in order to make it straight and manageable. She was ready to just get to dinner and celebrate with her amazing fiancé that this seemed an endless task but for the sake of Garrett and looking her best for him she plugged in the dryer with a sigh.

15

Once she finally finished her hair and applied a quick highlight to her eyes and gloss to her lips she stepped back to critique the job in the mirror. Just as she was doing what she assumed every girl does, finding the list that needs fixing, Garrett came up behind her with just the hint of a smile in his eyes. He put his arms around her waist and kissed the side of her neck.

"Stop trying to fix everything," he murmured into her cheek, "you look perfect and always have, there is no way to improve perfection." He could read her like a book.

"Yes sir," she gleamed with a tiny curtsey, "as you wish." She took his arm for balance and slid on her shoes. He escorted her to the door holding her coat for her. It was completely old fashioned and while she was extremely independent, she loved that he wanted to take care of her and thought that it was his job to do so.

He wrapped her up in another of his bear hugs kissing her deeply. Finally he swung open the door and held it for her as she headed for the stairs. Hailing a cab she looked down the street admiring the beauty of the lights glinting off the gently falling snow.

The ride shouldn't have taken long, the restaurant was only six miles away, but this was Chicago with Friday evening traffic. Every road was gridlocked. After inching their way through the maze of roads for nearly forty-five minutes, Kaylie and Garrett got to Café Le Amile. She was starving. The smell wafting from inside made her stomach rumble so loud she was sure others could hear it. The sensation was unbelievable. Unfortunately, so was the line out front. She looked doubtfully at the gaggle of people mingling around the front door.

Her disappointment was evident. Garrett could see it in her eyes. He walked straight to the door and held it open for her but she didn't budge.

"Garrett, this place is packed. There is no way we'll get in and I'm so hungry. Let's just walk down the street, there're a couple places down the way that I am sure aren't as busy." She started to turn away as she was still talking. "It was a really nice idea but we can try some other time."

Garrett caught her arm gently forcing her to turn around, guiding her toward the door. Resignedly she entered. She looked around almost sadly at the gorgeous décor. It was warm and charming with lots of cherry wood and red tablecloths reflecting the sensual energy from the fireplaces around the room. Though separated in spots for intimacy it was one large room filled with the general rumble of conversation punctuated with occasional laughter.

She turned around and saw Garrett in front of the host's stand most likely asking about any openings. She knew there wouldn't be so she walked over to get him.

"…window table." The host was finishing writing something down.

"Yeah I think that she would like that." He saw her coming and put his arm around her shoulders. "Good news baby, our table is by the window overlooking the park."

"Our table?" She was so confused it didn't register right away.

"Yeah, for the reservation. I asked for a nice table because we're celebrating but they really took care of us. They gave us the park view. Great isn't it?" His smile was almost as warm as the room itself. She couldn't believe it. Not only did he know she was getting the solo but he went out of his way to make this the most magical night he possibly could for her. Her love for him was indescribable and the depth of his love never ceased to amaze her.

She took his extended hand as they followed the host to their table. She glanced out at the amazing winter scene in the park. It was gorgeous but nothing compared to what she had sitting here right in front of her. It was just so typical Garrett to go overboard like this. When he proposed he used the cliché of spending the rest of his life making her feel as special and loved as he himself felt when he was with her. She knew that men said stuff like that all the time but he had spent the last year proving it to be completely true.

The most incredible part was that all he had to do was be there to make her feel loved and special. They were always competing in a silly game of who could spoil the other more. She knew the game was going to make their upcoming wedding the most wonderful night of either of their lives.

He watched her lovingly from across the table then reached over, lacing his fingers with hers. They looked over the menu and ordered wine along with their entrees. They made quiet conversation while the entire evening seemed to be passing like a dream. They talked about her solo and his ideas about promotions for the recitals. As usual talk turned to their wedding both exclaimed excitement and disbelief that it was only six months away.

The food was exquisite; the service exemplary, and as dessert was winding down she just knew she was in heaven.

"So do you think the reception food will taste that good baby?" she asked.

"I have a feeling it won't matter since we'll be so busy hugging people and dancing and of course kissing to the sound of clinking glasses we won't do much more than nibble," he laughed. "But I am sure it will be great. We tasted so many caterers that I'm positive we got the best in the entire Chicago area. In fact, we probably…" he was cut off by the sound of his cell phone ringing.

"Hello?" He paused, his brow furrowing as he listened. "I thought that was next week."

"Honey, what is it?" She could already tell it was work. That look on his face meant he was going to have to go in tonight.

He held up a finger signaling he would tell her in a moment. "Uh huh. All right well if Jason is that crazy about it I guess it's better that we just knock it out. Yeah ok." He sighed. "I'll be there as soon as I can." He ended and looked at her.

"I know; you gotta go in. I'm guessing this means no second dessert at home?" she said with a sexy little smirk.

"Oh god baby, you have no idea how much I would love that, but.."

"I know, I know. From the sounds of it your frantic boss is pacing a hole in his office floor."

"I will make this up to you."

"There is no way you could ever do more then you already have. And you have nothing to feel bad about." She still couldn't believe everything he'd already done. "Just go and I will see you when you get home, unless you want me to come hang out with you at the office."

"No hon, go home and rest. You've had a long day and tomorrow is one of the few that you can sleep in. I'll be at work until late I'm sure but will get home as soon as I can. Tomorrow, I promise, breakfast in bed."

"Just get home safe babe. That's enough for me." She leaned over and kissed him.

He agreed and after paying the bill he signaled for cabs out front. She got into the first one waving off his attempt to give her money for the fare. Blowing him a kiss she watched him jump into the second taxi that quickly pulled out and headed downtown. She leaned back in the seat with a sigh and closed her eyes waiting, for traffic to lighten so she could start the journey back home.

The heat of the cab was broken by a burst of icy wind as another passenger jumped in the back with her. She bolted upright glaring at the intruder. He was a lot to take in. She was immediately pissed off. How dare he interrupt the end of her wonderful night?

"Hey, what the hell do you think you are doing? Get out!" she yelled. "Didn't you see there was already someone in here?"

He just looked at her with dead, hollow eyes as though he didn't hear her and was just noticing for the first time he was not alone. Even when his eyes locked on hers he registered no emotion. It was terrifying to not be looked at but more looked through. Kaylie felt her skin crawl as he continued to stare.

"I said get out, what is the matter with you asshole?" He just wouldn't move. She reached over and pushed his grimy shoulder trying to get his attention. At first there was nothing but when she tried again he grabbed her wrist hard and twisted it. She cried out making the driver turn around to see what was happening behind him.

"Hey buddy, let the lady go!" he yelled. No response. "Hey! I said let her…" he was silenced by a flash of metal in the cold light from the street. The man had a gun. All of a sudden the man smiled. That was far worse than the empty stare. She struggled to free her arm but his grip tightened. The pain was enormous.

"Drive." It was obviously directed at the cab driver but he never diverted his eyes from hers. The taxi didn't move right away so, still without looking away, the dirty man slammed the separation window with the gun. That was all it took. The car leapt into traffic and began weaving through the rest of the cars. As soon as they were moving he released Kaylie's arm. She backed up against the far door.

She wanted out of the car, away from this lunatic. Looking at him horrified her but she found that she couldn't look away either. He was chillingly hypnotizing. Every detail of his disgusting image was burning itself into her mind. The way his stringy hair hung in his cold dead eyes. His skin hanging off his pointy cheekbones, streaked with age lines. He appeared in his mid-fifties, he also may have been homeless based on the smell of him.

Stained jeans and black combat boots matched well with the camouflage jacket over what may have once been a white shirt but now had dulled to an ashy gray. Everything had holes and reeked of urine and exhaust. His large hands were scarred. The black nails were chipped. His fingers held the gun loosely but still had a scary kind of control. She could feel the world flying by outside the cab.

Kaylie finally tore her eyes away from him long enough to see the blur of cars and landscape as they flashed by.

She peered around the driver and saw that they were only going 40 mph but it felt much faster when watching everything go by. She focused on the passing scenery. The realization dawned on her that they were heading toward her home. Fear washed over her again as she thought about this maniac learning where she lived.

Her street had been the last instructions given to the driver other than to drive so he must have just instinctually headed there. Thinking fast she tried to figure out if she would be able to outrun the crazy man in her dress or if she would even have the chance to make it out when the driver stopped. And of course what if he didn't want the driver to stop at all? What would he do then?

"Wwwhere are you going?" she stammered.

"Away." For a minute that was all, then "taking care of business and going away."

"Please let me go. I promise I won't say anything about you."

"Shut up bitch, I don't care about you." Kaylie didn't doubt that for a second. The way he looked through her as though she were invisible scared her to her core. The driver had said nothing but must have heard the exchange because he glanced in the rearview mirror, catching Kaylie's eye. Silently she pleaded with him to not let him see where she lived. At first nothing happened but then he made an unexpected turn away from her building, instead heading toward the highway. So far they had only encountered green lights but up ahead there was a stop sign and as he slowed the psycho with the gun erupted.

"Don't stop man, or I swear it'll be the last thing you ever do."

"Stop sign sir." There was a quivering in his voice. Kaylie could see the bead of sweat making its way down the side of his face.

"Just drive. Seriously, I will kill you. You wouldn't be the first one tonight." There was no explanation beyond that. The driver clearly believed him because the speed picked back up and he breezed past the stop sign without a second glance. They were only a block ahead when the night was illuminated with flashing red and blue lights. An officer had witnessed the ignored stop sign and was trying to pull them over. Again the driver began to slow; once more the madman hit the window with his gun.

"Do you really think I'm joking? Do Not Stop!" He roared the last part making Kaylie's heart skip a beat. The sirens started and the driver's eyes shifted in the rearview mirror. She could see he wanted to risk it and stop for the officer but as the person locked in back with the monster she really hoped he wouldn't do it.

"Pull the cab over," came the blaring command from behind them. "This is the Chicago Police Department. Pull to the side of the road now."

"Please sir, I need to pull over for the police. We won't say anything about you, just let me stop."

"No." He looked completely calm but there was no mistaking the tone in his voice. They were coming up to the highway entrance. She was terrified if they got to higher speeds the police might try to spin them out like she had seen on all those car chase shows Garrett loved to watch. She looked out the back window. The lights had multiplied as more officers joined the chase. God, how she wished they could see and hear what was going on inside.

The demands were coming more and more over the loud speakers. The freeway entrance was getting closer. With every foot the taxi went forward her heart sped up. The driver was trembling too. He began to sweat harder making a small river down the back of his neck. His white knuckles were shaking on the wheel. She was shaking herself. She was pressed so far into the door that she though she might simply become a part of it.

The car slowed one more time. The driver had decided to take his chances and let the cops come to the car. She could see the highway entrance at the bottom of the hill they just crested and was thrilled they weren't going to end up in the high-speed chase she had been envisioning. The crazy guy was sitting there looking at her. This time he was seeing her. The alertness that had come over his face was frightening to say the least. With the nose of the car pointing down toward the highway, the brakes screeched to a halt.

Without ever taking his eyes off her, he raised the gun and shot the driver behind the right ear. The shot was deafening in the confined space. As the driver slumped forward Kaylie could hear herself screaming. It sounded terrible in her head but the man with the gun was just smiling. For the first time she saw that he was missing most of his teeth and his wide gummy smile was just as creepy as everything else about him.

She was shaking worse than ever. After a moment she felt something sting her eyes. Reaching a trembling hand to her face she felt the hot sticky liquid. She looked and saw blood on her fingers. Shifting her eyes for just a second she saw that when he pulled the trigger the window had shattered. While most of it had gone forward to the front seat part of it had blown back at her and cut into her face.

There was a pinpoint of wind hitting her as well. She hesitantly turned away from him long enough to see that the bullet had gone through the driver's head and crashed through the windshield. The wind was coming through the hole. She also realized they were moving again. She hadn't noticed it right away but now she could see when the driver fell forward he hit the gas again. They were barreling toward the on ramp and picking up speed as they rushed downhill.

The police were following suit, heading down after them. They were still yelling but she could no longer make out the words. The nightmare had taken over. She felt numb. There was no one controlling this rolling deathtrap as they headed straight down into Friday night highway traffic. She sat staring out the front of the car starting to cry. She was going to die with this man and she didn't even know why.

She heard a loud pop. The car pulled violently to the right. She would have been thrown into the side if she hadn't planted herself there at the beginning of the ride. He tumbled forward, falling into her lap. He pushed himself up then glared out the back. The rumble from a flat tire muffled any other noises and she realized that the police must have shot out a tire.

She only had a moment to think about it before the front of the car collided with the sloped shoulder next to the entrance ramp. The car launched into the air, the impact making the doors burst open. Kaylie was thrown straight down with a bone jarring force. From her vantage point she saw the car flip onto its left side then its top as it rolled and slid downhill sending up sparks from the pavement. The crunch of metal was terrible. When everything stopped moving she tried to get up.

She couldn't move. She tried again but nothing in her body listened to the commands given by her mind. The police cars were stopping, surrounding her. She could hear them rushing toward her. Voices all around her were making a murmur but she couldn't make out any of it. All she knew was that the lunatic with the gun could come for her or the officers at any time. She wanted to yell for them to watch out but she couldn't make a sound. The darkness was closing in around her.

Kaylie made one last ditch effort to scream or move but her body had given up. She could see the blood running across her eyes and could feel it all over. Shadows ran all around her. Someone was talking to her but it was all just white noise. Goodbye solo she would never perform. Goodbye perfect night that never got the chance to end in Garrett's arms. Garrett, oh god. Goodbye love of her life. She had loved him from the moment they met and with the thought of never seeing him again her body gave up a single tear. It escaped her eye and coursed through the blood and dirt on her cheek making a single clean streak as the blackness took over.

Chapter 2

BEEP. BEEP. BEEP.

"… deep lacerations…"

"…compound fractures to the…"

BEEP. BEEP. BEEP.

"…going to need immediate…"

"…may be permanent…"

BEEP. BEEP. BEEP.

"…such a shame that she…"

"…probably will never…"

Kaylie kept fading in and out of consciousness. Her exhausted brain was growing more and more frustrated by the scattered pieces of conversation she was picking up. She wished she could focus enough for them to talk to her instead of just about her. Kaylie did a small scan of her body. She could hear things happening around her so she knew she could hear. She wasn't dizzy, though her eyes were still closed. She didn't feel any pain so they must have given her some intense medication. Or maybe she was actually fine. It could have been one of those miracles she read about where people go through terrible events but walk away without a scratch. Something else kept tugging at the back of her mind but she couldn't quite grasp it.

She tried to sit up or move her arms or something to get the attention of the shadowy figures encircling her but for some reason her body wasn't responding to her commands. She closed her eyes and tried again, but still nothing.

BEEP. BEEP. BEEP.

God that beeping was annoying. What the hell was that anyway? The more she tried to find any pain but couldn't the more she was sure everyone was talking about someone else. The nurses and doctors seemed to be describing injuries she knew couldn't belong to her. It felt like a nightmare. For some reason she was in this weird room surrounded by the people she couldn't quite make out listening to them talk about someone else. Then it hit her; this must still be part of the dream. That's why she couldn't feel anything. That's why she could only see shadows.

BEEP. BEEP. BEEP.

She focused all of her dreaming energy, putting as much force as possible into it and heard herself yell, "Hey!" In any other circumstance the wide-eyed stare and gaping mouth of the nurse peering over the edge of the bed would have been comical. Right now though it seemed very important to Kaylie to wake up from the nightmare so she could finally be free. Between the cab ride and now the hospital it would have been the worst thing that could happen to her if it were real. She blinked several times to try focusing her vision on the nurse before she again said, "Hey."

"Doctor, she's awake." There was a tiny bit of panic in her voice. From the corner of her eye Kaylie could see the exaggerated arm movements as the nurse gestured toward her. She closed her eyes trying to pick up the conversations that now seemed all around her

"...x-rays are showing multiples in the left and two separate in the right." Multiple what?

"I would be shocked if she's ever able to again." Ever able to what? This was maddening. She opened her eyes again but was bombarded with three faces all closely studying her. She took a deep breath. With a great deal of concentration she steadied her voice to be as clear as possible when she asked, "What happened?"

The medical faces conferred silently over her still unmoving body then disappeared from sight. She tried to turn her head sideways to follow the oldest one but was bungled in her effort by something soft but stationary. This hindrance was the final straw. She felt the tears of confusion and frustration well up and overflow. It was all too much.

If this was just a bad dream, why couldn't she wake up? And if it was real, why couldn't she feel anything? Then an even bigger question emerged in her mind, where was Garrett? If she really was in the hospital, had someone called him to let him know? She was about to give up when a movement at the bottom edge of her vision made her take a second look. From where she was stuck she could just make out the hair but it was unmistakable, Garrett. Kaylie's labored breathing tightened further as the realization sunk in. If Garrett was there, everything was real. It had all been real, and for some reason she still couldn't feel her body.

"Garrett?" She squeaked it out. Somehow over the beeps he heard and came up to her field of vision.

"I'm here baby, don't worry. I'm not going anywhere."

"Where is here? What happened?" Her voice was hoarse. He winced as she spoke. She could see him trying to push the worry from his face but his eyes betrayed his attempt.

"You were in a car accident honey." He leaned down and kissed her forehead.

"I was? It was real?" Her foggy recollection seemed like the memory from a dream. She had been sure none of it was real. At least she kept telling herself that in case she could make it true somehow.

"You remember what happened?" He asked, looking hopeful. Why would he want her to remember something so horrible? "Are you sure?"

"I remember bits and pieces but there are a lot of things I don't understand." She took another deep breath. It was exhausting just trying to explain all of the things she didn't know not to mention get answers to the questions swimming around in her head.

"What don't you understand baby?"

"Why can't I move or feel anything? Did they give me medications that made that happen? How long have I been here? How long have you been here? What happened to the crazy guy? Is he dead? Are the doctors talking about..." she trailed off when he put up his hand.

"There's a lot going on honey but as soon as the doctors know something definitive they will come talk to us I'm sure. We will get everything figured out." He was trying to sound soothing but she wasn't interested. His comments felt rehearsed.

"How long do I have to be here?" She pressed.

"Baby, you need to calm down. You're really hurt and my guess is you're going to be here for a while so let's just wait and see what the doctors have to say."

She didn't respond. She was running back over everything that happened that night. From getting into the cab and being joined by the scary smelly man, to seeing the gun and taking off on a run from the police against her will. She remembered every detail but wasn't sure if that would matter since she also remembered the way the car had flipped over her and crumpled on the road. She knew the driver was dead and imagined the psycho must be too.

"Did the police say what happened to the guy that caused the accident?"

"The cab driver?" Garrett looked confused.

"No the homeless looking guy that was in the back with me. He shot the driver, it was awful." She felt the tears coming again. He was still looking at her confused. The sad look on his face was starting to make her blood pressure rise. She hated when people gave her that pitiful gaze.

"Kaylie honey, there was no one in the crash but you and the driver. I'm sorry to say he died in the accident but luckily you survived."

"What are you talking about? There was a nasty smelling man that jumped in the taxi with me. He is the one that made the driver run from the police and when the driver tried to stop he killed him. He also said he killed someone else tonight." She could see his disbelief and her frustration went over the edge. "I am not crazy!" she screamed.

"I know you aren't crazy, but you have been through a terrible ordeal tonight. I'm sure you are overwhelmed right now. You're just in shock but soon you will feel much better then everything will be clearer for you." He sounded so certain but she knew she was right. He hadn't been there. Besides the police must have just forgotten to mention that part to him when she was brought in, or they chose not to for some reason. Either way she had more important things to take care of at the moment. She stared at Garrett. His hair was disheveled, his red-rimmed eyes had a glazed look to them, maybe he was the one that was overwhelmed. Once she got out of the hospital she would make sure she knew what happened to that maniac, it seemed impossible he could have survived.

BEEP. BEEP. BEEP.

She had managed to block that obnoxious noise out but now it seemed to overpower everything else. She felt like she was drowning in an audible pool of beeps. Nurses and doctors reentered her field of vision but they were just mimes performing behind the orchestra of medical equipment. It was going to drive her mad if the beeping didn't stop.

"Oh my god, make the horrible beeping stop, please." She yelled it as loud as she could but no one appeared to have heard her. She yelled again and still, no response. Was it all in her head? Maybe she already was crazy. Her head began to spin as the tears continued to flow.

A hand brushed her cheek. She saw Garrett was wiping away her tears. She wanted to smile but was worried her mouth wouldn't do what she told it to do. He was saying something but the machines were still invading her ears. She struggled to listen and eventually his voice broke through.

"Kaylie, the doctor is here and needs to talk to you. Do you want me to stay?" It never crossed her mind that he wouldn't. She opened her mouth to tell him that but as before, her voice betrayed her. When nothing came out she nodded as much as she could. Out of sight his fingers entwined with hers' and she looked at the stranger in the white coat, waiting for the diagnosis.

"Akaylia Jean Reynolds?" the doctor asked.

"Kaylie." She always corrected people, Akaylia was the name her mom had given her trying to be unique but she liked Kaylie. It fit her better.

"I am Dr. Bendfints. I have been going over your information. We need to talk a little about what we've found and what you may be feeling." The doctor didn't miss a beat when she corrected him. "First we would like to take the opportunity to say it is great to see you up and we are very optimistic about you making a strong recovery."

Strong recovery? Why didn't he say full recovery? It seemed odd. At the same time it chilled her to her core that he took the time to be so careful with his word choice. What the hell was wrong with her? She took him in as she waited for him to continue. He was easily in his sixties with a mop of white hair and the little spectacles you always expect from the elderly. His white lab coat was a little too big and looked slightly faded. She wondered if he wore an old coat out of comfort or for the effect.

The doctor was standing there patiently, watching her with a glimmer of concern in his hazel eyes. The lines on his face deepened as he waited. His apprehension seemed to grow as well since she hadn't responded. "Miss Reynolds, did you hear me?"

"Yes."

"So you understand then?"

"No. Why did you say make a strong recovery? What is wrong with me, physically?"

Dr. Bendfints hesitated for a minute, exchanging looks with the other medical staff in the room. It infuriated her. They were treating her like a little kid that might overreact to bad news. She wasn't planning to throw a temper tantrum, all she wanted was to know what the hell was going on and exactly how long until she could get out of here. She had a lot to do between the wedding planning and dance rehearsals. She needed to get back to her real life.

"You have extensive damage to many areas of your body Miss Reynolds."

"Kaylie," she corrected him again.

"As you wish. Kaylie. You have multiple fractures in both of your legs. You have three broken ribs and one of them is pressing into your lung. You have a very serious concussion. While you were unbelievably lucky to not break your neck, you do have a severe sprain. Your back also has a serious strain. We believe you have herniated more than one disc in your spine. You have over a dozen cuts and lost quite a bit of blood. We have several treatments that we will be implementing including surgery on your ribs; recovery is going to take a long time and will not be easy. There is a very strong possibility that some of your physical injuries will result in permanent limitations."

There it was; the truth. She was hurt in a way that could be permanent. She'd known that she was bleeding because she remembered the sting of it running into her eye at the accident but she still was having a lot of trouble believing things were as bad as she was being told. If things were actually that bad, she should be in terrible pain. she still didn't feel much of anything.

"I don't believe you." She said as defiantly as she could. There was a sinking feeling in the pit of her stomach that told her he was telling the truth, but she couldn't shake the issue of there being no pain.

"Honey, he's just doing his job. He has no reason to tell you anything other than the truth." She glared at Garrett shutting him down.

"I don't feel any pain so I don't believe it. There is no way I could be broken and useless without being in horrible pain, duh."

Sarcasm and disdain dripped from every word. She glanced at Garrett. He was clearly hurt by her tone. She knew she should be sorry but right now she didn't care. Her attention was on the doctor and his mixed up information. Maybe he was looking at someone else's chart. Yeah, that had to be it.

"Kaylie, you can be stubborn all you want and the denial is perfectly normal. You've been through a traumatic experience. It'll take time to sink in completely. The most important thing right now is that we need to get you started on these treatments. You need to understand what we're doing and why. You're in shock right now so your body is separating from the pain but believe me, you are going to break through that and the pain will come." His even matter-of-fact tone was aggravating. All she wanted was to go home. "I know you want to go home and get back to your life but it's going to be a long road."

It was like he was reading her mind. She felt her hand get squeezed and shifted her eyes to Garrett. He was giving her a pathetic hopeful gaze but if she had been able to control her body she would have yanked her hand away. She didn't have the patience to deal with him right now.

"I am not interested in your treatments. I need to go home and get back to my life."

"Baby, I think this is going to be part of our life for a bit. I know it's hard but we are in it together. I am sure we can get through this. We just need to be strong."

"Oh shut up! None of this happened to you. You're fine. You can leave whenever you want. This happened to me and I am the one that has to deal with it." She snapped at him. How could he be so stupid? How could he be so selfish? He was perfectly fine but they were saying that she had serious injuries and some of it could be permanent. What if she couldn't get to rehearsal and Sabrina gave her solo to someone else? What if this stopped her from getting another solo?

That was when the biggest question hit her. It was like being run over by the cab and left for dead all over again. What if she couldn't dance again? That was crazy right? Dr. Bendfints never said that; but he did mention permanent problems. "How long until I can get out of here? I need to get back to my rehearsals."

The question didn't seem to surprise anyone in the room but the lack of response certainly shocked her. She expected either an immediate answer or at least that nervous look between the nurses and doctors again but nothing happened. All in the room simply looked at her and waited.

"When the hell am I getting out of here?" she demanded, much more loudly than she intended but no longer caring. She sounded hysterical because she felt hysterical. Her breathing was labored and she had begun to sweat. Her rapid heart rate told her that her anxiety might be taking over. She took a couple deep breaths but nothing changed so she gave up. She went back to focusing on her desperate need to know when she would escape.

Garrett looked at her lovingly. He quietly opened his mouth to say something but her icy glare stopped him. He stood up, dropping her hand to the bed, before he stalked out of the room. She turned back to the gaggle of medical staff watching her.

"Well?"

"Miss Reynolds," she started to correct him but he held up a hand to cut her off. "I understand the frustrations you're feeling, Honestly I do. I know the desire to get back to normal. Unfortunately you are going to be here with us for a while and once you do go home it won't be over. As I had mentioned it is highly possible that you may have some permanent damage. Depending on how serious things end up being, you may not dance anymore. At least not in the same capacity you have up to this point."

"Sir," she said as calmly as she could, "I am a dancer. That is who I am. It is not just what I do but what I exist for." She was shaking as the depth of his words sunk further into her psyche.

"You have danced. It is something very important to you and I am not trying to downplay that at all, miss. But you have many things to live for. I know your friends and family will want to help you as you move past this to begin the road to recovery." With that he turned and began the parade of men and women exiting the room. The last nurse adjusted the bed so she was sitting up a little past half way. She could now see the cold empty room she had been abandoned in.

If he is right and dancing is over, then it's simple; my life is over, she thought. She couldn't understand the ignorance of that horrible man telling her to move on. Acting like there was anything other than dancing for her. What the hell was she supposed to do now? She was so deep in her thoughts she didn't notice Garrett peek in to check on her. He watched until the medication kicked in again settling her into a troubled half sleep.

Chapter 3

Tossing and turning in her limited mobility, Kaylie drifted through a semi-conscious world trying to get a firm footing and understand what was happening around her. In this parallel plane she was walking but only through still scenes of her nightmarish cab ride. The spotlight of her memory illuminated every glaring detail. Strolling past the shot of the man climbing into the back seat with her she felt her skin crawl again.

She attempted to pause, but her dream self kept moving forward. She passed the scene of him yelling at the driver while she pressed her body against the door. She wanted to go back but the momentum of the dream propelled her on. She could feel her sleeping body aching from the tossing and her mental state shake from the image coming into view.

There, she saw with horrifying clarity the moment the gun went off. The flash from the muzzle, the shattering window, finally the driver being thrown into the steering wheel. She wanted desperately to turn away, to run away. It was incredible how powerful her need to escape was becoming. It compared only to the actual moment now frozen in time before her.

Her racing pulse and labored breathing set off her monitors bringing a nurse bursting into the room. The young woman grabbed Kaylie, squeezing her arm and yelled into her ear.

"Wake up miss!" There was no break in the fearful mumbling. "Miss Reynolds! Wake up!" She grasped Kaylie by the shoulders, making sure not to move her stabilized neck. She ran her hands down her right arm shaking and squeezing as much as she dared.

"Make it stop, I don't want to see anymore," Kaylie cried, hot tears streaming down her cheeks. "Please, oh god, just make it end."

"It was just a dream Miss Reynolds, you're fine." She was trying to sound comforting but Kaylie wasn't hearing any of it. She continued to cry, but now that she was waking up she could feel the nurses hands on her and she began to struggle and fight to get away.

The nurse tried at first to hold her down. She was determined to keep Kaylie in place. But the stronger she held on the more Kaylie fought. Finally she released her grip and that did the trick. Kaylie stopped struggling but her sobbing remained. By now Garrett had been roused from his dozing in the waiting room and came in to try to calm her. She saw him and for a moment reached for him but when she saw the bandages on her arms she stopped, looking around the room in a panic. The beeping machines and smell of antiseptic all came rushing beck to overwhelm her. She covered her face with her hands as the tears began once more.

Garrett stopped short when she began crying again. Hiding her face made him feel like she was hiding from him. He came to her side, reaching for her hand, but she turned away. He stroked her arm instead trying to find the right words to comfort her but nothing came. He just wanted to let her know he was there. The nurse came over, leaned down and reset the alarms on the machines.

"Miss Reynolds? I need to check a couple things then I'll let you get back to sleep. Can you look at me please?" At first there was no response. Kaylie sat, sunken into her pillows, still hiding in her hands. Her hair, dripping from tears and sweat, clung to the sides of her face and gathered at the nape of her neck. "Miss Reynolds?"

"Go away."

"I will let you get back to sleep in just a minute. Just please let me examine you. Then you can rest again, I promise."

"Did it look like I was sleeping well, bitch?" Kaylie snapped.

"Kaylie!" Garrett was completely taken aback by her outburst. He had never heard her talk like that. "She is just doing her job. You don't need to talk like that."

"Oh go to hell. You have no idea what is going on or how I feel. Just go home, you don't need to be here. I'm the one stuck here, not you."

"I'm here to help you, honey. You're not alone. I'm just trying to help." He shifted his weight as she glared at him. He still couldn't find the right words to say or a way to make the sadness in her eyes go away. He felt helpless.

"Yeah, yeah, yeah. You think you're helping but all you are doing is bugging me." She sighed and turned her head away so he couldn't see the fresh tears spilling down her cheeks. Totally dejected, he got to his feet and went to the door. He hesitated for just a second as he looked back over his shoulder at the woman he loved.

"I'm going back to the waiting room after I grab some coffee from the cafeteria, please let me know if there are any updates." He kept his eyes on Kaylie even though she refused to make eye contact. He waited a moment more but when she said nothing his shoulders slumped and he turned out of sight. She could hear his fading footsteps echoing in the hallway. She was surprised to find she felt some relief he was gone.

He was only there to try to take care of her but she knew he could never understand what she was going through. He couldn't help and she didn't want to be a burden to him. If she couldn't dance any more than life as she knew it was over. She would be useless to him. He would probably leave her anyway so may as well get used to the idea of being alone from now on. Why would he want to be with someone who never even got to be a "has been"? She was simply going to end up a "never was".

At least being on her own she didn't have to worry about letting anyone down. She felt like this was the beginning of the end, She was really not looking forward to dealing with all the shit the doctors were going to put her through before she was able to go home and suffer alone in silence. Garrett may as well just leave and start to get on with his life.

The nurse finished her exam without a word then left. Kaylie lay in the glow of the fluorescent bar mounted over the bed. In the harsh light she felt like she was having an out of body experience. The most recent dose of painkillers kicked in making her feel like she was floating above her body. She watched with a combination of horror and fascination as the scene that had just been performed in her room now played again in her drugged up mind.

She saw Garrett, at least the highlights of his performance. She watched the entrance with concern on his face, the pain as she rejected his need to help and the sorrow upon his exit. She then reran the big moments with the nurse and finally watched from her own point of view and realized with mild amusement that she was completely indifferent to the entire scenario. It was like watching someone on TV deal with fictional problems.

She was now a character in her own life, and apparently one she cared very little about.

Chapter 4

The next morning came and with it so did a seemingly endless amount of doctors, nurses and questioning members of the public. Most of them were there to explain what part they would be playing, so they thought, in her recovery. All of them asked the ridiculous question of how she was feeling today. Then they all got "down to business". The nurses came and went, giving medications or checking readouts from the machines. They pretty much faded into the background after the third round. Kaylie barely noticed them.

The doctors presented the results of the tests they had been running from the moment she was brought in before they announced their individual treatment plans. Each of them seemed so proud of what they showed her. After their explanations they left but not before reminding her of the long hard road that lay ahead while also letting her know they would get through it all together; whatever. The most annoying was the psychiatrist. She popped in to say they would be having daily talks. She also wanted Kaylie to know she was there if she or Garrett needed anything. That was it, already phoning it in, great.

After they finished, Garrett came in briefly to ask if there was anything he could do and to tell her he loved her. She knew he meant well and of course she loved him too, but all she could manage was a mumbled thanks with a forced smile. He kissed her cheek squeezing her hand when he left, telling her he would be back later. She nodded numbly.

There was quiet for about an hour so she had settled into her pillows letting the soothing warmth of the morphine course through her veins. Sam Waterston was busy preparing the case against yet another accused murderer on Law & Order and she was floating in a sea of indifference when there was a knock on the door to her room. Her cloud faded away. She returned to earth long enough to recognize the blue uniforms entering her tiny haven.

She watched them warily. There were three men walking in a polite, single file line. As they made it further into the room she could see only one of them was in a police uniform. The other two wore suits and carried notepads. She wondered why they needed the uniformed escort. When they reached her they turned to face the bed, standing almost at attention as though waiting to be told to have a seat. She didn't oblige. The officers waited. She decided it would be fun to join the game so she straightened up, returning their gaze. The silent standoff probably only lasted twenty seconds but it felt much longer.

She gradually grew bored with the staring contest. She looked over them to the television and saw the jury deliver a guilty verdict. Good old Jack McCoy does it again. She smiled. It had been ages since she watched the show. She never had time to watch much television anymore. Of course the bandages and braces wrapped around her body suggested it might become a bigger part of her life again. She had nothing but time now. She lowered her stare once again to look at the officer directly below the screen. He was obviously the rookie looking easily fifteen years younger than the other two.

He tried to hold her gaze but within seconds was shifting his weight from side to side, staring at her forehead instead of making eye contact. He cleared his throat, looking at the man to his right. Ah, he must be in charge. Kaylie fixed her gaze on him. He shifted slightly as well. Finally after seeming to consider the alternatives, he broke the silence.

"Miss Akaylia Reynolds?"

"You already know who I am, what do you want?"

"No need for curtness, Miss Reynolds. I'm Detective Meyar and this is my partner John Rommel. We're just here to ask you some questions about the accident and see how you're feeling today."

She began laughing. She laughed deep and long. They were looking at her, could easily see all of her bandages. She was sure they must have also been to the scene of the accident. Yet here they were, acting like she should be happy and smiling, as good as new. The blank, innocent look on their faces was just too much. As soon as she got herself under control she regarded them but one look into their eyes made her start giggling again.

The officers exchanged glances. They were clearly uncomfortable dealing with the hysterical woman lying in front of them. She could see them dancing back and forth, still none of them had taken a seat. Gasping, she gradually got herself under control. The tears dried up as her breathing returned to normal. "You want to know how I'm feeling? Really? That is what you came here to talk about?"

"I know you must be in unbelievable pain. We just wanted to check on you, to see if there was anything we could do to help."

"No. There is nothing you can do. My life is over, so just ask your stupid questions and get out of here."

"Well we wanted to know what you remember, if anything, about the accident." The older detective finally took a seat in the chair next to her bed. He took out a small recorder. The younger two flanked him, still standing at attention.

"Do your lap dogs need to stand there like that?" She couldn't help herself.

"Miss Reynolds, you don't need to say things like that." His steady gaze was trained on her. He gave her a gentle smile. He clicked on the recorder while also pulling out a pen to go with his notepad.

"Whatever." She rolled her eyes and turned her head away. "If you want to ask me any questions, then make them go away." He didn't move. The statues standing behind him remained in place. She turned back, giving them all her sweetest smile. The rookie leaned back. She locked eyes with him, keeping the smile that held

41

neither warmth nor sincerity. It was a definitive way to show that she meant what she had said.

After what was probably another full minute Detective Meyar waved them away. At his signal they turned, marching from the room. The door clicked closed behind them. Once they were alone Kaylie fixed her glare on his calm, inquisitive face. "Ask what you need to then leave. I want to be alone."

"Ok, I can do that. Do you remember anything from the accident?"

"Yes."

"Ok, Miss Reynolds, I need you to give me the information you remember and not play any games. This is very serious and the more information we have, the better we can figure out what happened so we can finish our investigation."

"You don't need to spell it out for me like I'm a child. My God, do you really have nothing better to do than bother me?"

"Miss Reynolds, I understand you're upset. We just want to put everything together and make sure everyone is on the same page. Can you please tell me what you remember?"

"Fine. I remember the accident and the terrible man that caused it. He was horrible. He was smelly and scary. And it's Kaylie by the way, stop calling me 'Miss Reynolds'."

"Alright, Kaylie then. I understand what you went through was traumatizing but I didn't notice anything scary about the driver. We did, of course, see the bullet wound in his head. The lead officer has reported seeing the flash from the shot. Why did you shoot him?"

"What the hell are you talking about? I didn't shoot anyone. The driver wasn't the scary one; it was the awful guy in the back with me. He was the scary one. He smelled like urine. He kept demanding that the driver speed up and wouldn't let him stop. He didn't show much emotion but the rage he did show scared the shit out of me."

42

"Miss Reynolds, Kaylie I'm sorry, we have gone over the scene. We found you unconscious on the outside of the accident perimeter. We also discovered the driver dead on arrival in the front of the cab. The car was completely totaled but as far as we could tell there wasn't anyone else in the car at the time."

"That isn't possible. I remember everything. I'm telling you he was there. He hijacked my cab; he killed the driver. He caused the accident. I was just stuck along for the ride. You have to believe me, he was there!"

"We have all of our best people working on this. If there really was another person in that car, we will do everything we can to find him. Please, can you describe him for me?"

Kaylie launched into a full description of the man that changed her life. She described him and every move he made with exacting detail. By now she had fresh tears spilling down her cheeks. She gave up trying to stop them. As her story progressed she could hazily make out a slight change in the detective's demeanor. He changed from a demanding insensitive jerk to an actual human being. He kept the recorder on and though he barely spoke, once she started, he kept looking at her waiting for and expecting more.

It felt wonderful to get it all out. The metaphorical weight was being lifted off of her. For just a moment she forgot her diagnoses. She got all the information out she had stored inside. She didn't even realize that it had been bothering her that much until she opened the floodgates. When she finished she took a long, slow, deep breath.

The final image of the car crumbling in a heap on the road and the screeching of the metal as it slid on the asphalt filled her mind. It sent a tremendous shudder through her entire body; the shaking made every inch burn with pain. The detective winced in sympathy for her as he got to his feet.

"I am truly sorry for you Miss, umm Kaylie. I can't begin to imagine what you've been through and the long road you have ahead of you."

"Oh my god," she moaned. "I can't take anyone else talking about the long road ahead of me. There is no road; my life is over. The road goes over a cliff and comes to a violent and terrible end." She covered he face with her hands. She had finally stopped crying but the frustration brought it all back on again. The tears came so easily. She was completely exhausted from trying to control them. The detective reached over and tried to pat Kaylie on the back but quickly realized there was no safe place. She was gone again; lost in her pain. He wanted to say something but she wasn't paying attention anyway so he pulled a business card out of his holder and left it on the table next to her bed.

She didn't know how much time had passed since he had left but she knew he left the card. She reached over, picking it up, she studied it closely as though it held some answer to a question she had yet to ask. The only thing she found waiting for her though was his phone number and a hand written note saying to call if she remembered anything else. On the other side was his name, Detective James Meyar. She knew as long as they were investigating she would hear from him again but it was definitely a name she would rather have forgotten.

The investigation. The thought burst into her mind. He mentioned they were investigating and that if they found another person had been in the back with her they would bring him to justice. How could he look at her and say if? How could he have ever thought she was the one who killed that poor driver? How could they not know there was another person in that godforsaken taxi? Of course there had been someone in the back with her. It was ridiculous to think anything else. She knew that if they had the best people working on it then it would turn up but she was amazed that he hadn't been there. He had to have died in the crash; no one could have survived what she saw.

As she was contemplating the confusing situation, Garrett poked his head in to check on her. She sat staring at the wall going over and over the car ride in her head. She had no idea the man that had so recently been the whole reason she existed was even in the vicinity. His heart sank into his stomach when she didn't bother to look up for even a moment. He withdrew from the doorway. He honestly believed they would get past this whole situation. He knew whether she accepted it right now or not that she would go down the recovery road and eventually be all right. His pain came mostly from the long road he would be traveling down himself and the fact that no one realized what he was dealing with.

He was suffering too. Just because he was not the one physically injured, he was passed over for treatment and concern. Allowing a moment of selfishness he hung his head as he leaned against the wall. He was going to have to be strong for Kaylie and he would be strong for her but he hoped eventually someone would be there if he needed strength himself. The detective had left Kaylie's room but not the hospital, and now he approached Garrett.

"Sir, I am Detective Meyar. I'm investigating your fiancés' accident."

"Yeah, I saw you and your colleagues coming out of her room." His voice betrayed him but he straightened up, shaking the officer's hand. "Was she able to help out much? Did she remember anything?"

"Yes, she 'remembered'." The air quotes he made immediately tugged on Garrett's last remaining nerve. "She remembered another person being there with her and the driver."

"She had mentioned that to me too, but I thought your people determined she was the only passenger."

"From what we've gathered so far, that is accurate, yes."

"Is it possible that someone else was there? She seems so sure."

45

"We're looking and we will find them if they were there. But I have to ask; does Kaylie have rage issues? Is there anything you can think of that would make her snap and injure the driver?"

"What?" Garrett was completely shocked. "Are you seriously asking me if my fiancé is capable of causing the accident that injured her and killed the cab driver? Honestly?"

"She seems very certain that there was someone else there but none of the officers on the scene saw this mystery man. They only found Mr. Kashim and Miss Reynolds."

"Kaylie," Garrett automatically corrected him. He was deep in thought now. He knew that there was no way she could have caused something like this. It had injured her. It could have killed her. Not to mention it could possibly cause her to give up dancing permanently. Dancing was her whole life; he thought and was surprised by the slight bitterness that came with the realization. She was everything to him and dancing was everything to her. "There is no way she could have done this."

"Well if you remember anything," he pulled a wrinkled business card from his pocket, "please don't hesitate to call." With a final glance he turned on his heel and strode away. When he was about halfway down the corridor Garrett broke his gaze, turning his attention back to the closed door of Kaylie's room. It was the first time he had felt anything but love and concern when looking at it. While both of those emotions were there, floating right below the surface was something darker. He, for the first time in his entire life, felt the tiniest bit of satisfaction about an injury.

The thought that she might never dance again didn't make him happy but the fact that it would result in him being number one with her instead of coming in second place to her career brought a hint of a smile to his face. He knew he should feel bad about that and a part of him did, but the rest of him enjoyed the thought. He absently flipped the detective's card in his fingers as he turned down the hall. He followed the same path Detective Meyar had making his way out of the hospital into the cold night air.

Tucking the card into his wallet he took a deep breath, looking around. He spotted a line of taxis by the main door and began to trudge towards them but was stopped by the thought of Kaylie's accident. Surely the crazy man that had hijacked her cab was long gone, probably crawled into some nearby alley and died from his injuries. He was certain that the drivers were just there waiting to make their next trip and record the next fare but the uneasiness was enough to make him change direction. He walked the two extra blocks to the station for the L.

The wind cut through his jacket like a knife. His ears felt as though they might jump off his head and abandon ship but he was still lost in thought so much of this passed unnoticed. The train pulled in, slowly opening the doors. He felt the rush of warm air greet him as he stepped on board before taking a seat. It really was going to be a long hard road for both of them. He knew he would have to be her rock, but the recent epiphanies that had come to him tonight made the work seem much easier to bear and the payoff well worth the effort. He smiled more broadly, leaning back against the wall.

He took a deep breath then let it out with a grateful sigh of relief. He had planned to run home and grab a shower along with a change of clothes tonight then make his way back to the hospital but he decided he would shower and stay in instead. Watch some television; maybe make a decent dinner. Sounded like a great plan to him. Maybe even take a quick look at the revised presentation notes for the campaign. He had received the email notification on his phone but the file was too big to open so it had not been his priority until now.

The train chugged on, jerkily covering the distance between the hospital and home. When he reached his stop, Garrett climbed to his feet pulling his coat a little tighter around his body. He stepped onto the platform making his way to the stairs, the same ones Kaylie had skipped down barely forty-eight hours ago. He descended to the street. Once there he shuffled through the sludge covered sidewalks to his building and waited for the elevator. Everything seemed a milestone for him tonight. As he hung up his coat and collapsed on the sofa he realized just how tired he actually was.

His eyes moved from the doorway to his bedroom and the shower within, then jumped to the kitchen where a filling meal could be made then fell on his computer, quietly holding his productivity. One more sigh before he snatched the remote off the coffee table. He clicked on ESPN but before the commercial break was even over he was deep in a restful sleep.

Chapter 5

The next morning Kaylie opened her groggy, sleep-filled eyes and was ambushed by an obnoxiously cheery face. The woman sitting by her bed gave her a huge smile. She looked far to chipper for any time of day let alone morning. Kaylie glanced at the nightstand and saw the clock read 6:52. *Oh my god*, she thought. *I don't even wake up this early on weekends without an alarm.* Yet there was someone sitting there, silently smiling at her. It dawned on her that the woman might even have been there for a while, watching her sleep. That was creepy enough to make her shudder a little.

She did look slightly familiar but Kaylie figured she was probably a nurse, there had been so many of them in and out of her room by then she forgot some of their faces. She scanned the files in her head as finally settled on a memory of a woman popping in to tell her something then leaving again. *Ah*, she thought, *the therapist returns.*

Her psychiatrist sat there, the annoying smile never wavering as she observed her. Kaylie shifted on the bed, waiting for the questions to begin. She imagined she would have to talk about how she was feeling, what she remembered about the accident as well as how she felt about the future. The answers were ready and waiting, she was terrible, yes she remembered and there was no future so therefore reason to talk about it.

"Are you hungry?"

"What?" That wasn't on the list of questions she had expected.

"I asked if you're hungry. The hospital has great breakfast food. I can grab you something or we can call down and have it brought up, kind of like room service."

"Umm, ok. I guess I could have a bagel or something."

"Is that all you want? Really? I'm thinking eggs and bacon myself."

"Yeah, sure, that sounds good. Whatever you're having I guess."

"Maybe fruit plate instead. Toast and coffee. Be healthy, you know?"

"Ok, we can do that. Are you getting it or do you want me to order it, or what?"

"I think you should decide which breakfast we should have then we can order and have it sent up."

"I said I would eat whatever you wanted." She was ready to just get this chat started. The sooner it started, the sooner it would be over. She really thought the bacon and eggs sounded good but she wanted to get the right thing so she waited to be told what the doctor wanted.

"Man, I am hungry."

"So what do you want me to order?" This was weird. Why not just say what she wanted so Kaylie could order? Or just order it herself? Her question was greeted with a smile and patient silence. Ugh, this was so frustrating. She was the one that mentioned food. Because of that, now Kaylie could feel her stomach rumbling. She didn't care which meal was for breakfast; she just wanted to eat.

"Are you not feeling like breakfast? I thought I heard your stomach rumbling but might have just been mine."

"I'm hungry. I just don't know what you want me to order for us."

"I told you to decide. We can order whatever you want."

"You want me to decide for both of us?"

"Yes."

"Uh, I don't know. What do you think?"

"I am not going to decide for you Kaylie. You decide what we're going to eat, otherwise we are going to be hungry."

"What if I pick something you don't want?"

"Well pick something and we'll see."

50

"Wouldn't it be easier if you just…"

"Kaylie." Her voice immediately stopped all conversation. Then she commanded, "Pick something."

"Umm." She felt tears stinging the corners of her eyes. How dare someone who works with mental conditions put her through this emotional torture. She fought back the tears, mad at herself for getting so upset over something so stupid. "Eggs and bacon?"

"Are you asking me or telling me?"

"I was asking if that sounded good."

"Just decide."

Kaylie flailed her arms in frustration. This woman had been sitting here bugging her for almost an hour. She was a therapist, wasn't she supposed to be helping her? All she'd done was drive her crazy about breakfast. "Fine," she sobbed. "Fine the eggs and bacon."

"Sounds great." The doctor reached over, grabbed the phone and ordered while Kaylie got herself back under control. It didn't take long for the food to arrive. Her therapist dove in; eating heartily while Kaylie watched nibbling in silence. The pain and medication for it made eating difficult but she tried. After all it took long enough to get the breakfast situation settled.

Once they finished her psychiatrist got up and pulled on her jacket. Kaylie looked at her, amazed. She was leaving? They hadn't done anything. "Good work today Kaylie. We have already made some progress. If you want to talk again just have me paged. Just ask them to talk to Cindy, ok?"

Kaylie nodded but said nothing. This was the oddest session she could ever have imagined. She expected to be harassed about how she felt. She pictured crying about her ruined future while insisting there was no issues with her parents or her childhood. Instead she argued about breakfast. Cindy felt they had made progress. She was just in the middle of considering that maybe Cindy was a psych patient herself when she realized she had been told to call her Cindy. Not doctor something or even Miss or Mrs., just Cindy.

While considering this interesting situation, it also came to her that she had only referred to her as Kaylie. She never said Miss Reynolds like everyone else did. She barely had a moment to let this sink in any deeper though because suddenly Cindy swept back into the room. She plopped a notebook and a couple pens on her stomach.

"I almost forgot to leave these with you. I swear sometimes I would forget my head, you know?" She laughed as she turned, heading back out the door. Kaylie stared after her too stunned to speak. Even after the click of the door signified no one was coming back in to bother her. She picked up the notebook and examined it.

Basic college ruled notebook with seventy pages under its simple black cover. The pens were also unremarkable. Plain blue ink pens with tops to clip them to the cover if desired. She opened the cover and leafed through the first dozen or so pages when a Post-It slipped out onto the bed.

For your thoughts and questions. That was all it said. So Cindy wanted her to write things down so they could go over them at their next session. Well good luck with that. She didn't need to do homework. She also had no intention of assisting with this weird therapy. Cindy hadn't even cared enough to explain what she was supposed to do, just left a ridiculous little note. What if she hadn't looked through the pages? She never would have found the instructions.

An idea came to her then and she yanked the top off one of the pens, tossing it off the side of the bed. *Why do you think this is a good idea?* She jotted it down appalled by the horrible scratching her handwriting had become from the painkillers and restrictive bandages. Then another question came. *How could fighting about breakfast be progress?* She laughed as a few more came to mind getting added to the list as they sprung into her mind.

52

After filling the first page front and back with questions about the silly tactics from her useless session she put the book aside. She turned on the television. Flipping through channels she settled on Lifetime, busy showing a marathon of Project Runway. She had never been into the show, having no time to stay caught up but right now time was one thing she seemed to have an endless supply of.

She watched a couple episodes and obliged a few nurses that came in to check on her. She listened half-heartedly as the procedures and tests for the next day were explained then around five tried ordering spaghetti for dinner. It came in a small dish with a side of buttered toast, no garlic bread, with some chocolate pudding for desert. As the final episodes wound down her half-eaten meal was picked up and she began to feel tired again.

She yawned deep, rubbing her eyes. She yelped in pain when her engagement ring snagged the bridge of her nose. She stared at it for a while. She felt ashamed she had gone the entire day without noticing Garrett wasn't there. Her guilt gradually turned to frustration and anger though because he hadn't come by to check on her. It wasn't like him. He was everything to her, she would give up anything to make him happy and he always told her the same thing. She loved him with all her heart; she thought he knew that.

Her tears began anew as she thought about how she loved to dance for him. When she was on stage people always said she lit up, looking like she was exactly where she was supposed to be. She was the happiest dancer in the world. But what none of those people ever knew was that, for her, the only person in the audience she could see was Garrett. He was her inspiration.

But where was he? Why hadn't he come by to see her? Pain and confusion coursed through her. Her fingers twitched in the folds of her blanket. She couldn't think of a single reason he wouldn't come by. Then in a heartbeat she was struck by a horrifying thought, what if something happened to him? He was bound to have gone home to change at some point. What if he got in a cab and that crazy guy had survived? What if he hijacked Garrett's taxi as well?

She cried. It came harder each time. One of the nurses came to check because her heart monitor began to beep, signaling a significant change in her heart rate. She mistook the tears for pain, giving Kaylie another dose of morphine. Kaylie attempted to wave her away but she was crying so hard she couldn't get the words out. Before she felt under control again the nurse had disappeared. The heat of the medicine was rushing her into a drugged semi-conscious state. *Garrett*, she thought, *where are you? I love you so much, please be ok.* With that her body gave up the fight. She closed her eyes finally drifting off to sleep.

Chapter 6

Garrett had slept late and made himself a huge breakfast when he finally woke up at one in the afternoon. He stretched out on the couch while watched Sports Center for a couple hours then eventually wandered over to the computer. He reviewed the presentation notes and sent back his suggestions. He returned a few emails before doing a load of laundry. It was a productive day considering the last forty-eight hours he had been dozing in the waiting room and checking on the fiancé that barely noticed his existence.

He loved her, God knew he did, but right now he was also incredibly angry with her. On top of that he felt enraged with himself for being mad at her after everything she had been through. With his head spinning from all the contradicting feelings at the moment, now would be a bad time to visit her. He had called twice that afternoon to check on her, thanking the nurses for their updates. He also called Sabrina and left a message as to what had happened even though he was sure she already knew.

The story of the accident made the front page in the paper so he was certain that most people in the greater Chicago area were aware. He also called her parents to give them the update while assuring them he would check in often to let them know about any changes. Both her mom and dad were closing in on retirement age. When he called to tell them about the accident her mother had broken down, insisting on leaving work to come take care of Kaylie herself.

Garrett knew he was persuasive. He also knew Kaylie's dad was a reasonable man functioning more on logic than emotion so he had appealed to him that he had things under control and would act as liaison between them and the hospital. He didn't have the heart to tell them that her injuries were most likely career altering or that he was avoiding her because of jealousy over her preference to dancing. However he let them know about the treatment plans and that she had been awake and talking. He closed saying she was strong, a fighter. They would get through it together and were looking forward to a visit very soon.

Hanging up he had taken a shot from the liquor cabinet. He rarely drank. She never did but with everything going on and having to relay information to her emotional mother, it had been a taxing conversation. He considered for a minute then took a second shot before putting the alcohol back on the shelf. He missed her and called her room but there was no answer so he rang the nurses' station to request a final update. The head nurse told him she had been in pain so they gave her a dose of morphine. She told him Kaylie was resting comfortably. He knew morphine upset her stomach but it seemed unhelpful to point it out right then so he thanked her and hung up.

He went into the bedroom to get ready for bed figuring he would call it an early night then go see her bright and early. After brushing his teeth and climbing into bed he opened the newspaper, scanning the articles for something to take his mind off the cover story.   On page four a headline caught his eye. There had been a man robbed at gunpoint then left in an alley to die only two blocks from the restaurant. The man had been thought dead at the scene but had been revived and was in critical condition at the same hospital where Kaylie was being treated.

Wow, he thought, *it had been a terrible night for a lot of people.* He wondered how the man was doing and something about the story tugged at his mind. With the hospital's policy to not share medical information about patients he doubted he would be able to get any information from the nurses about the man's condition but he figured it couldn't hurt to ask. He made a mental note to talk to someone tomorrow and see if there was anything he could learn. It

56

was really bothering him that there was something else pertaining to that story he felt like he should know.

He reread the article focusing on the description of the man that had been seen running from the alley. The paper said he was wanted for questioning as a witness but Garrett was sure it was just code for 'he was a suspect'. The witness believed he was homeless and said he had heard what sounded like a car backfiring. After the man was found it was assumed he actually heard the gun firing instead. That nagging feeling wasn't going away but it wasn't clarifying either. *Oh well*, Garrett thought, *I will sleep on it and ask about him tomorrow. I'm sure the police are hopeful he will make it. Maybe he can identify the guy that tried to kill him.* He yawned hoping for answers as he fell asleep but nothing clarified in his dreams.

Chapter 7

While Kaylie was having her interesting first therapy session, and Garrett was sleeping late, the lab technicians working for the Chicago Police Department were busy taking apart the destroyed remains of the taxi. It had been impossible to determine directionality of the shot that killed the driver from the window because it shattered in the accident. They were also unable to decipher prints or DNA deposited in the backseat for indication about if there may have been another person in the car at that time.

The techs weren't even aware they were trying to determine if there had been. All they knew was there were questions and they needed answers. Working diligently, they tested and studied every aspect of the car. They recorded their findings, checking periodically with one another to verify and uncover information linked together from different aspects of the scene.

The report from the chasing officers stated that the car had stopped just over a hill. There had been what appeared to be a shot fired then it had begun to descend the hill picking up speed until it veered off the road and crashed. There was evidence of all of that but the big question of why the driver had failed to stop before, and why he then was killed still remained. Both officers in the front vehicle during the chase described the car windows as cloudy. From the heat inside the vehicle it was impossible to see anything happening. When the subject of another passenger arose they both offered the same conclusion, if there had been another person, they would have been found at the scene.

In the morgue nearby, doctors were busy performing an autopsy on the driver. It was discovered that the trajectory of the shot had come from over his right shoulder. That didn't rule out Kaylie as a possible shooter, she could easily have shot him from that angle while sitting right behind him. However, there were no burns on his skin from the shot itself nor was there any gunshot residue found. There had been the window between the shooter and the victim but some of the residue would have been on the glass that stuck in his skin if the shot had been fired at close range.

It would have been extremely awkward for her to sit behind him then twisted her wrist and arm to hold the gun far enough away to get this particular angle. It was, of course, possible that she had been sitting on the right side. The police couldn't identify where she was located because of the fogged up windows. She would have been much better situated for the shot from that position but when the car had started to flip and the doors burst open she came out with the door in a single movement. That action led everyone to believe she had been sitting right next to it if not against it at the time of the accident. There was not a second of delay as there would have been if she tumbled from the passenger side and she was not thrown from the right door even though it had popped open as well. But again it was noted there were a few seconds between the shot and the time the car veered off the road.

Writing the autopsy report, the coroner called Detective Meyar to update him on the findings. The detective thanked him for the information and disconnected. He then filed the report contacting the liaison for the lab to let the techs know he was finished so they would have a full view for the report. He didn't know Kaylie as a person, but if his findings were able to help find the person that had done this to her then he would be satisfied. *Assuming she is innocent,* he reminded himself.

The technicians continued to toil away looking for clues, now also seeking evidence of a second passenger. As the car was pieced back together they discovered residue on pieces of the divider window behind the front passenger seat confirming the origin of the shot. They also worked fervently on reconstructing the puzzle that was the window itself.

With the final fragments being put in place they were able to make out the large hole the bullet created and determined it was a .38 caliber. All of the information continued to be compiled in their reports and Detective Meyar was once again called to update.

He thanked them for their hard work. As he hung up something started to nag at him. He couldn't quite put his finger on it but there was something odd about the findings. He let it roll around for a bit then it struck him, there had been a shooting not far from the restaurant Kaylie left immediately before her ride from hell. That incident had the same caliber weapon according to the report. He flipped through his notes and found the description of the man seen leaving the scene then called the hospital.

Kaylie was sleeping the nurse told him; it would be better to come by tomorrow. She was going to be in tests and therapy for much of the day but the nurse assured him they would find time for him to talk to her. Thanking her he jotted down the times she gave him before putting the notebook away. He smiled, so she had been right all along. She remembered everything. The smile slowly faded, he just hoped she was going to be all right.

Chapter 8

The following morning Kaylie awoke with a start. She squinted against the bars of sunlight streaming through the open blinds. As her eyes adjusted she felt the hairs on the back of her neck standing at attention, she felt she was being watched. Shifting her gaze left she let out a small, startled scream when she saw the smiling face of Cindy. Damn that woman, she did it again. She was watching her sleep, probably coming up with more stupid exercises that didn't do anything for anyone. It was so creepy.

But then she got up and walked over to the door, when she opened it Kaylie was relieved to see breakfast had already been ordered so they weren't going to be playing that stupid game again today. She ate in silence for a while before regarding Cindy with weary eyes as she waited for the fun to begin.

"How's Garrett?" Cindy asked like they were girlfriends just catching up.

"I don't know, I didn't see him yesterday." She was surprised how sad that made her. Of course she missed him, she loved him, but honestly, could she not go a day without seeing or talking to him? It appeared not.

"I see. Did you call him?"

"No." Cindy seemed to consider this for a moment.

"Why not?"

"I'm the one in the hospital, he should be checking on me."

"But he has things going on in his life too I'm sure. Might be nice if you check on him every now and then." That made sense but it also made Kaylie angry.

"You think I am so self-involved I don't know that? He is everything to me. I love him more than anything else in my life. It's just that I am the one suffering right now so I should be the focus."

"Ok."

"What does that mean, ok?"

"It means alright, I got it, no problem, I understand."

"You meant something else by it, didn't you?" Kaylie's eyes narrowed as she watched her therapist shovel food into her mouth.

"What do you think?"

"That is the most frustrating thing you therapists do, your patient asks you something and you just say 'what do you think' or something stupid like that."

"I see."

"Oh my God, stop that."

"Ok, well breakfast was good but I have a bunch of paperwork to do today. You have your notebook so just jot down any thoughts or questions you have and we will talk about them later." She stood up, putting her sweater on. "Have a good one."

As she left Kaylie stared after her. What the hell was that? They didn't talk about anything; all she did was basically call Kaylie a bad fiancé. How dare she say that? It was ridiculous, she cared about Garrett and he knew exactly how she felt. Besides she was his whole world too. It only made sense that he would check on her. So why hadn't he?

She grabbed the notebook and filled nearly three pages with her irritations when there was a gentle rapping at the door. Garrett, she thought, thank god you're here. "Come in."

Detective Meyar nudged the door open a crack and peered in. He was greeted with a heavy-hearted sigh before she went back to scribbling her thoughts on the waiting pages. He clomped into the room, taking a seat next to her. He leaned over trying to read some of what she was writing but she noticed and snapped the book closed.

"What do you need detective?"

"Our lab has been going over the evidence collected at the scene of the accident."

"And what did they find?"

"It appears, though inconclusive at this time, that there may have been another person in the vehicle besides you and the driver."

"I know, I already told you that."

"Yes, you did. I know you started to describe him for me but I was wondering if you could tell me everything you remember about him." She narrowed her eyes and watched him for a minute.

"Why?"

"We are just trying to make sure we have all information possible." He opened the notepad and reread the description he already had then flipped to the next page while he awaited her answer. Slowly she told him everything, the smell, the long stringy hair, his clothing, everything she could remember. She closed her eyes. He was sitting right in front of her again. The detective asked about the gun. She hadn't had more than a glimpse of it but she told what she knew. When she finished he snapped his booklet shut just as she had when he came in. "Thank you."

"Can I ask you a question?"

"Sure, what's on your mind?" He asked, getting to his feet.

"Did you find anyone else that had been shot that night?" He was clearly taken aback.

"Why do you ask?"

"When the driver tried to stop for the police, the crazy guy said he had already killed someone and it wouldn't bother him to do it again." He dropped back into the chair and stared at her.

"Why didn't you say something about this sooner?"

"Because you didn't even believe he was there, why go any further?" She wicked away a quick tear. "You found someone else didn't you?"

"Yes. He was shot in an alley not far from the restaurant."

"So he was telling the truth, he had already killed someone."

"Not exactly."

"What do you mean?"

"I really cannot discuss an ongoing investigation, all I can tell you is that a man was shot but survived."

"He survived? Did he fight back?"

"We don't know, we are still looking into it, but he is alive. Now that we know it could be the same person we have more information to try and catch this guy." He got back to his feet making his way to the door. He turned back and for a moment looked more like a caring parent and less like a member of law enforcement. "Take care Kaylie, we're going to do everything we can to catch this monster."

Monster. That was the best word she had heard for him yet. She watched him leave then looked at the notebook. Having the detective believe her had taken away all of her anger. She still felt like writing but without the rants she wasn't sure what else there was.

The door pushed open again. Standing there, framed in the light from the hallway was her prince. Garrett had come back and she knew everything would be ok. She smiled at him but he just returned her gaze. She felt her smile fade some as he took a silent seat next to her. Without a word he turned on her television. He sat there flipping through channels, noticeably not talking. Tears welled up along with her frustration when he continued to not ask how she was doing. Her hands balled into fists as she opened her mouth to tell him to get out when Cindy's observations jumped into her head.

"How are you doing Garrett?" She asked with all the concern and sincerity she could. She was shocked to see him turn to her and finally smile.

"You really want to know how I am?"

"Of course, I love you." Could Cindy be right? Was he dealing with stuff too?

"I'm tired honey. I'm worried and exhausted and a little depressed."

"Depressed? Why?"

"When the doctors came in they explained that your injuries were severe. When they told you dancing might be over, you said life was over. It is just a job Kaylie."

"I know that. It's just all I've ever known. I'm not good at anything else so I didn't think you would want me anymore. Losing you would kill me."

"You thought your life was over because you thought I would leave you?"

"Yes." He smiled so big she thought she could count all his teeth.

"Baby, I am never going to leave you. Besides dancing is just one of the things you are good at, trust me. You're beautiful, intelligent and extremely talented. Everything is going to be just fine." She breathed a sigh of relief that things were on more stable ground with Garrett, but it did little to quell the disappointment still brewing inside her. Of course he was her world but dancing was a part of her. She knew he was wrong about everything being ok.

They spent another half hour together talking while flipping through the channels just enjoying each other's company. He brought Wendy's with him. She nibbled on some of his fries even though she wasn't very hungry. They tasted so much better than the terribly bland hospital food she was expected to order three times per day.

A nurse hesitantly cracked the door to let them know she needed to take Kaylie down for an MRI in just a couple minutes. He smiled as he tossed the wrappers in the trash. Leaning over he gave her a sweet long kiss and as much of a hug as was possible with the bandages she still had on. He promised to come back in a few hours to see her after he stopped by the office. He also promised he would call her parents to update them about how she was doing. He was being so great it brought a tear to her eye. She quickly rubbed it away, God she was sick of crying.

Her tests passed uneventfully and she was quickly able to get back to her room hooked back up to the machines. The most important one in her opinion was the one giving her the painkillers. It was amazing just how much they helped. The doctors and nurses told her that they would be weaning her off of them as soon as the intensity lessened so she could begin to recover on her own. The thought of giving up the comfort of the medication made her heart race. Her nerves got the better of her so even though she wasn't sure what her pain level currently was, she kept claiming an eight or nine out of ten. That way the pills and injections kept coming on schedule.

She didn't want to tell anyone she was exaggerating the pain because they might call her an addict, or worse yet, stop giving her the drugs. She wasn't addicted, she knew; just smart enough to make sure she was taken care of until she was ready to take over getting better on her own. It was genius, she decided, if you really thought about it.

Once she was back on the machines and had her most recent doses, she told the nurse she was struggling to sleep so she gave her another pill to help. Kaylie gave her a grateful smile and thanked her as she hungrily snatched the pill and water. After letting the relaxing effects of the pill take control she called Garrett. She told him she was exhausted from the tests so she was going to get some sleep. He sounded disappointed but said he loved her and would come by tomorrow.

She turned on the television and found Hell's Kitchen. She laughed at the over-inflated egos of the wannabe chefs as they fought through yet another disastrous dinner service. After seeing Chef Ramsey break the heart of one more hopeful she drifted off into a wonderful drug induced sleep. She had no dreams that night and no one came in to wake her up and check on her concussion. Everything was great for the first time since she was brought in.

Chapter 9

That same day, on the other side of town, Detective Meyar was busy as well. Armed with the information of another possible passenger along with a half dozen uniformed officers he combed through the accident scene. Just off the side of the on ramp was a small wooded area leading to a park. After scanning the road for a third time, he ventured into the brush and almost tripped over the evidence he needed that he was on the right track. Lying in the dirt was a .38 caliber pistol full of pine needles and mud.

His excitement nearly got the better of him. He caught himself just before he wrapped his bare hand around the grip. He pulled his hand back snatching a pen from his pocket, using it to lace through the trigger guard. It was dirty and definitely plugged at the end of the barrel but he was completely positive this was the gun used in both the robbery and the car crash. He stumbled back out of the bushes handing the weapon to the nearest officer to have it tagged before he ran back to the park.

A few broken braches and some drag marks through the dirt gave the distinct impression someone had crawled or pulled something through this area recently. It hadn't snowed since the night of the accident so nothing was there to cover the tracks. Detective Meyar followed the path into the clearing of the playground. There was a flurry of footsteps there, mostly from children but some adult sized ones roamed the area as well. Unfortunately it was impossible to distinguish the ones from the trees from the parents of playing kids.

He walked the perimeter twice before he found long shuffle marks leading back toward the street. However once they reached the sidewalk there was no sign of direction. The pathways here were shoveled and salted regularly. He looked up and down the quiet road making a mental note of the four large condo buildings within walking distance of the park. He strode back to the officers where he gathered them up for canvasing assignments. After dispatching them with the description Kaylie provided he took the gun and photos he collected and left to drop them off at the lab.

Chapter 10

Kaylie had gone to sleep early, with the lack of usual interruptions she awoke early as well. She grabbed the notebook, writing for almost an hour before she heard Cindy's voice greeting people as she came down the hall. Rolling her eyes she set the notebook aside. She made herself a promise she wouldn't get upset or frustrated with the therapist today. She would simply listen, get through the dumb session, and then she could get on with her day.

Cindy breezed into the room meeting Kaylie's gaze with that annoying smile she always seemed to have. It didn't appear to surprise her at all that Kaylie was already awake. She just took off her jacket and opened a folder. She scanned whatever was in the file quickly then put it on the table next to her and sat down.

"So, how are you feeling today?" She finally asked the question that Kaylie had been expecting from day one.

"Fine."

"Is that all?"

"Yes."

"Ok. So you aren't in pain anymore? Impressive." She grabbed the file again, clicked her pen so she could make a note.

"I am still in a lot of pain but it's ok cause they are giving me medication."

"Uh huh." She didn't bother looking up.

"What is that supposed to mean?" Kaylie snapped, instantly breaking the pact she made with herself.

"Nothing, I was just acknowledging that I had heard you."

"Oh. Well it sounded like you were judging me for still taking medicine. I am in pain so I'm allowed to, I am not addicted or anything."

"Ok." She kept writing. This was infuriating. The tears were welling up again so she turned away crossing her arms over her

69

chest as best she could. The next ten minutes were spent in silence with only the sound of Cindy's pen scratching across the paper.

"So, how do you feel about starting physical rehabilitation tomorrow?"

Kaylie turned back, stunned. No one told her anything about that. They had run some tests for range of motion. They had thankfully taken off the itchy neck brace, but nothing was mentioned about rehab. "What are you talking about?"

"I will be coming by later in the day for our sessions because you'll be doing rehabilitation for forty-five minutes every morning.

"I wasn't told about that. Why wouldn't I be told about that?"

"Well I reported back that you don't like being in charge of things so they could feel free to just tell you what was happening, or if they wanted just come get you. I told them you would follow along." She bowed her head and continued writing.

Anger overwhelmed Kaylie. She slammed her hands down on the bed. Cindy didn't jump, just looked up innocently waiting for the explanation. "Why would you tell them something like that? It isn't even true. I make decisions. I choose things for myself all the time. I am the one in charge. You're stupid if you think anything else so I shouldn't even listen to you, nobody should."

Cindy stopped writing. This was exactly what she had wanted, an emotional response instead of the planned answers she had been getting. "What do you think I was doing during our very first session?"

"Arguing with me over breakfast for no good reason."

"I didn't argue with you Kaylie. I asked you to make a decision about what to order for breakfast but you tried to defer to me over and over. You were never comfortable deciding for either of us. It's clear you're a follower and that is why you feel everything is over. You're the one that will have to decide to get better but you don't have the courage or ability to stand on your own two feet so to speak."

70

Kaylie was silent. This was ridiculous. "You know nothing about me," she whispered. "I am perfectly capable of making decisions and I will get better on my own, just to prove you wrong."

"Ok, well I have another appointment so I will check in with you tomorrow after rehab to see how you are feeling." She brightened up again. "Have a good one."

She gathered her belongings then left without another word. Kaylie was fuming and hurled one of the pens after her. The notebook caught her eye. She tore it open nearly ripping the cover off in the process. She wrote all of her frustration about how she was underestimated. Her rants progressed to her anger followed by the pain she was in. Then after filling pages with her frustration about physical ailments, she ranted about the monster that caused it in the first place.

This opened the floodgates. She turned the page and began writing feverishly about the night she was injured. She wrote out every detail of the night, the man, and his actions. Everything she saw, everything felt, all of her fears became a part of her memoir. She stopped only long enough to press the nurse call button in order to retrieve the tossed pen. Once she had it the writing began anew. The next time she stopped it was because she had actually gotten the entire night down in black and white.

Glancing over at the clock she saw it was after three in the afternoon. She had been working for well over four hours but felt satisfied it was all there. She had accomplished something. Massaging her cramped hand she leaned back against the pillows taking a deep breath.

"Wow, you were really into that." Garrett observed from the side of the bed. The sound of his voice made her jump so much she yelped in fear and pain. He squeezed her hand and smiled. "Sorry, I was pretty sure you didn't notice me but you were so focused I didn't want to break your concentration."

Catching her breath she smiled back. "Its ok, I was just writing about the accident. Don't want to forget anything that happened for when they catch that guy."

"That's a good idea. Where did you get the notebook?"

"My therapist left it for me. She is so stupid but at least I can write about how useless she is, that makes me feel better."

"Why do you think she's dumb?"

"She said something today that couldn't be further from the truth. She said I'm afraid to make decisions, that I don't like being in charge."

"I see." He folded his arms and thought about this.

"What is that supposed to mean?"

"Well baby, I can actually see it a little. You're very strong and more than happy to take charge when it's something easy like how to set up the furniture, even though you still ask me if I think it is ok. But what about at the studio? You're the only performer to not submit a choreographed piece to have considered for the show. You prefer to perform instead of create. But there is nothing wrong with that."

She was stunned into silence. He agreed with that moron? He thought she was weak, that she couldn't do anything for herself? Her eyes narrowed to slits. She looked at the wall, ignoring him. After nearly five minutes he gave up and kissed her forehead. She turned away when he whispered that he would stop by after work and see her tomorrow. She was shaking with rage as he left. Once again she threw a pen at the door. This time she chucked the dry one before grabbing the notebook again.

She delved into her anger again, this time about the lack of support from the man that was supposed to love and believe in her. How could he side with that ignorant woman? She was driven and ambitious, the only reason she didn't submit a choreographed number was that she enjoyed performing in them more. Besides it would take a lot of time to put a routine together. She thought he would have preferred that she spend her time at home.

She pushed the call button and steamed more irritations while she waited. The nurse came bounding in to answer the call but stopped short when presented by Kaylie's expression. Something about the pain on her face brought everything to a screeching halt.

"What can I do for you?" The nurse practically whispered.

"I need another notebook," she answered. She waved the original one in the air for emphasis. "This one is full."

"I'll see what I can find for you."

"Thank you, actually I may need a few of them."

"Let me check for you." She disappeared back out the door. Kaylie wrote on the cover while she waited. About fifteen minutes later the nurse pushed her way back into the room with an armful of notepads and spiral bound notebooks. She also had foreseen the possibility of dry pens so she brought a box of mechanical pencils and pens.

She set them down on the bed then stepped back quickly. "Is there anything else?" She inquired, still backing up.

"No." Kaylie watched the young nurse hesitantly moving toward the door. Why was she walking like that? The woman bumped the door and jumped, without taking her eyes off Kaylie she felt around then grasped the handle. She edged her way around to the opening to the escape of the hallway.

"You should be all set for a while." She practically yelled it as she ducked out the door. *What a strange person. She almost seemed afraid of me,* Kaylie thought. Well she would have to deal with that later, right now all she wanted to do was write her frustrations down.

She wrote and wrote; she complained about how no one believed in her. She vented about people not taking her seriously, believing she was a pushover. Garrett didn't believe in her, no one else came to visit her, the doctors and nurses barely spoke to her and even her therapist had no respect for her. And now, damn, the tears were welling up once again. She couldn't believe just how awful this all was. She couldn't move without pain. If the doctors were to be believed, there was a strong chance dancing wasn't going to be a part of her life much longer.

So she would be alone and have nothing. No support or way to release the anger about it. What a great day this was turning out to be. She wrote all day, continuing into the night. She finally stopped from exhaustion, falling asleep with her pen still gripped in her fist.

Chapter 11

Detective Meyar paced the length of the lab. He had personally brought in the gun and other evidence collected now he was anxiously awaiting the findings so he could get back out there to find the man that caused so much destruction. He checked his phone for the time. Instead he saw a notification he had missed a call. Scanning the log he saw the hospital tried to reach him and he instantly hit the return call button on the screen.

He was connected with the dispatcher and gave his information. She politely forwarded his call to the trauma ward. The few seconds it took for the doctor to pick up ticked by slowly. He checked the phone screen; saw it was only six seconds so far.

"Hello?"

"Yes, this is Detective Meyar. I received a call about twenty minutes ago."

"Ah, yes detective." The physician's voice was solemn. "I contacted you regarding Mr. Denton. He went into cardiac arrest. We were unable to revive him. He passed away just before I called."

"His injuries caused it?" Meyar already knew the answer but he just needed the confirmation.

"Yes sir."

"Do you know what happened?"

"There was internal bleeding. We didn't notice it at first; it was a slow leakage. When we located it we also discovered an aneurism that was inoperable."

"Why?"

"It was located at the base of the brain just above the spinal cord. We were unable to get to it. The arterial tear was also in the same area. It would have been too dangerous to attempt to remove the aneurism. By the time the bleeding was discovered it was too late."

"I see, well I know you did all you could."

"We did, let us know if you need anything else in regard to Mr. Denton."

"Ok, thank you."

They disconnected and the detective sat down on the lobby bench. He put his head down taking a deep breath. He and his partner were the first responding officers when Denton was shot. They were the ones that had radioed for the ambulance. He remembered going to the hospital, speaking to the doctors that night. He had been completely relieved when Denton made it through the night. He was in a coma but the medical staff seemed optimistic about his recovery, now he was gone.

Detective Meyar had seen many bodies during his years on the force. He had delivered the news to numerous families that their loved ones had passed on. It never got easier. He never wanted to hear the news that someone that survived an attack didn't make it after all. He sat upright and sighed. Now he was going to have to make the drive out to Denton's parents' place in Schaumburg. They were in an assisted living home and he was very concerned about what the news would do to them.

He had met Mr. and Mrs. Denton once already. The morning after the shooting he made the trip out to speak with them, to explain the situation. Upon hearing the news her son had been shot, Mrs. Virginia Denton had collapsed in a ball of tears. It had taken several minutes for her husband to calm her enough for Meyar to finish explaining he was in the hospital and though in a coma, would probably still come out of it. This glimmer of hope had been a miracle. Now he was dreading having to take it away again.

He checked the time once more then called his partner to update him on the situation. He appreciated the offer of company but told him to stay home and enjoy time with his family. After a few moments of superficial small talk he hung up. He gathered his coat and hat. This was going to be extremely difficult.

He started walking to the door when his sleeve was pulled. He whirled around, nearly knocking the meek lab tech to the ground. The young man jumped back from the hulking detective. The hand holding out the file for the detective shook uncontrollably. Meyar snatched it, examining its contents. His eyes grew wide as he continued down the page. The gun had been cleaned of mud and debris when it was brought in. While the elements had destroyed any chance of prints being lifted the lab still managed to match the weapon to an earlier crime.

He closed the file, tucking it under his arm as he headed out to his car. The drive passed far too quickly, even though he took back roads for a good part of it, so he could keep looking through the findings from the lab. Before he knew it he reached the nursing home. He sat in the vehicle staring at the main entrance. He checked his phone, getting to be kind of a nervous habit. Finally, he sighed to himself. He couldn't put it off any longer. He glanced through the file one last time then went inside.

Denton's parents were sitting in the common room playing cards with another woman. Detective Meyar took his hat off and strode over to them, determined to get this over with. As he approached Virginia looked up and waved. She lit up when seeing him but his expression immediately sobered the celebration. Denton's father, Brian, glanced back over his shoulder when his wife began to wave. His face fell when he saw the expression as well.

He staggered to his feet and grabbed Virginia, trying to support her even though he himself was barely able to stand. She said nothing just started to cry and shake her head. Brian looked into the detective's eyes. All questions he had were answered except for one, what happened?

"Detective." Brian said.

"I'm terribly sorry." He didn't need to make the announcement; the sobbing Virginia told him that.

"How did it happen? I thought the doctors said he was going to recover." Virginia curled up sobbing on the chair. She said nothing.

"They had run several tests when he was admitted but it wasn't until he had settled they were able to do a deeper MRI and CAT scan. Unfortunately they found an aneurism as well as a small leak causing internal bleeding at the base of his brain that was inoperable. Again, Brian I am so sorry."

"I need to talk with you about this more but I need to get Virginia back to our room first, please make yourself comfortable. I'll be back as soon as I can."

Meyar stepped aside. He felt his heart swell as he watched the hunched over man help his sorrow ravaged wife to their room. Once they were out of sight he took a seat in the corner of the room so he and Brian would have some privacy when he returned. Taking advantage of the moment of solitude he mentally went over the information in the file from the lab. The gun had been used three years ago in another robbery.

The other robbery had also been in an alley only five blocks from Café Le Amile. He was glad to know the gun had a history so he could track it. He was even more thrilled the lab recovered the serial number and was able to track down who the gun was registered to, a man named Kyle Marks. He purchased the gun eight years ago but had reported it stolen a month before the first robbery. At first the police looked at him anyway but quickly turned their attention to his estranged brother. Nick Marks was homeless. Kyle and his wife had taken him in briefly until he pawned their television for money to buy drugs.

Detective Meyar remembered reading about Kyle Marks and the brief mention of his wife Sabrina. The name hit something in the back of his mind but he couldn't quite figure out what it was. He knew it was something big though. Just as he was considering calling his partner to ask him to check into it, Brian returned and took a seat next to him.

The two men talked for a couple hours. Brian reminisced about his son. Some of his fondest memories involved how he had been involved in the arts. He was a music director for a dance company in Chicago, though he never could remember the name. He asked what he needed to do to get everything planned for a funeral. Meyar told him he would have someone from the hospital get in contact with him and would be of any help he could. After again giving his condolences and promising to do everything in his power to bring the man responsible to justice, Detective Meyar left. He rarely gave himself the privilege, but on the way back to his office, he cried.

Chapter 12

The next morning Kaylie awoke early to find the same hesitant nurse from yesterday standing in her room. She lightly shook Kaylie before telling her she had a visitor. Technically it wasn't visiting hours; even Cindy's obnoxiously cheerful face hadn't shown up yet. Then she remembered today she was supposed to do physical therapy so her session with "Miss Perky" wouldn't be until later.

"Who's here this early? And why do they get special treatment to come bug me before visiting hours even begin?"

"Because I know how to bribe the nurses." Sabrina burst into the room tossing a bouquet of wildflowers at her. Kaylie sat straight up at the site of her mentor.

"Oh my god, Sabrina!" Kaylie practically squealed with excitement.

"Yes, it's me, in all my glory." Sabrina laughed taking a deep, dramatic bow. Kaylie laughed right along with her. It felt good.

"So I give you a solo and you go and try to get yourself killed huh? That's not very helpful, hon. You need to get better so I don't have to give that solo of yours to someone else." Kaylie immediately started to cry. The site of Sabrina had made her forget all about the diagnosis for a minute but now having to tell her idol she wasn't going to be coming back, it all seemed like more than she could take. "What did I say?"

"Oh Sabrina," she wailed. "I hurt my back and neck. I fractured my legs. The doctors said I'll get better but that I'm not going to dance again. My life is over."

"The hell it is." Sabrina was indignant at the thought. "You have a million things going for you and if you think for one minute that someone telling you something makes it definite then you may as well give up right now. Now I don't want to hear any more about you giving up. I am going to be checking on you and I expect progress, understand?" Kaylie nodded and Sabrina stood up. "I can't stay just needed to come make sure you were alive and all. I will report to everyone that you are progressing so you better not make me a liar."

"I promise."

"I know you do. I'll check on you in a couple days."

"Thank you."

"Feel better, hon."

"I'll try, bye Sabrina." It was the fastest visit she had had but she needed to see Sabrina, it was uplifting to say the least. Still, she expected miracles. Didn't she understand that Kaylie was really hurt? How was she supposed to overcome the fractured legs or the herniated discs in her back? What about her ribs? She just didn't understand. Her frustration dissipated slightly as she yawned and glanced at the clock. It was only seven thirty in the morning; she was exhausted. She had been up writing late into the night and only got a few hours of sleep before Sabrina's abrupt visit.

She lay back and was asleep as soon as her head hit the pillow. Around her the medical personnel came and went, checking readouts or administering medication. At ten o'clock the shy nurse came back in to rouse her. It was time for her to go to surgery. She knew that she was lucky after such a horrible accident she hadn't broken any bones but now she had to wonder what surgery they were talking about.

"Surgery?" she asked clearing her throat and trying to get the sleepiness out of her voice. "I thought Cindy said I had physical therapy today."

"You're going into surgery this morning for your broken ribs. They are concerned now that you are moving a little more the one poking into your lung will puncture it."

"Why not do it when I first came in?"

"I'm not sure miss. I'm just here to get you prepped and taken down to the OR."

"Fine, whatever," Kaylie muttered. "So how does therapy work if I am supposed to have surgery the same day?"

"Your therapy is just an orientation. They're going to gauge where you are at and let you know what you will be doing. Also they will let you know some of the exercises you will be doing once you're sent home."

"Oh, Cindy made it sound like I was going to actually be doing the exercises today."

"Sorry for the confusion."

"Um, ok. I guess." She closed her eyes and massaged her temples. This was all so frustrating. "So how long is the surgery?"

"It should only be an hour, two at the most. Then you can come back here and rest."

"Alright," she yawned again. Actually the chance to sleep for another couple of drugged up hours sounded nice right now. The nurse finished checking everything then moved her IV bag to the stand on the corner of her bed and then wheeled her into hallway. There, waiting for her, was Garrett. He smiled and took her hand.

"Hey baby, how're you feeling?"

"I'm ok, just a couple hours then I'll be done."

"I know and it's a completely routine surgery, so no reason to be nervous."

"I'm not nervous, just tired."

"That's good. I will be in your room when you get done and I am planning to go with you to physical therapy so I can know how to help you."

"Thanks honey." She yawned again. He walked along with her as they made their way down the hall, taking the elevator to the surgical floor. Garrett kissed her as she was taken off to the OR then headed to the cafeteria to grab some coffee. An attendant tried to show him to the waiting room but he had had enough of them during the first couple days she'd been there. He politely thanked her but took his coffee and wandered back to her room to wait for her.

Kaylie never even saw the anesthesiologist; as soon as Garrett kissed her goodbye she fell asleep again. She never knew any of what was planned or happened during surgery but thankfully it was uneventful. She was back in her room in no time. Garrett was there watching television when she woke up. He immediately turned his attention to her ready to tend to her every need.

"I'm hungry baby." She mumbled.

"I may have something that will help you then hon." Garrett produced a bag from under his coat and she saw the golden double arches. It was greasy and unhealthy and it smelled phenomenal. She smiled as she sat up taking a long sniff. Her mouth watered for the cheesy, salty goodness. Reaching out for the bag she was almost giddy.

Garrett handed her the fries then put her burger on the napkin he laid out on the tray in front of her. He kissed her forehead as she devoured the French fries with almost record speed. It didn't take long for her to remove all trace of the fast food he smuggled in but he smiled his secret smile and she stopped mid-bite to look at him inquisitively.

"How was the food baby? I'm guessing pretty good since you're already finishing the last bite of it."

"Yeah it was great, can you get me some water?"

"I think I can find something for you to drink." He got up and grabbed a glass of water, but he brought it back and started drinking it.

"Hey, I'm thirsty." She reached for the water but he swatted her hand away. He grabbed something from the floor next to his chair and produced a cup. When he handed her the frost-covered cup she giggled. It was a chocolate shake. *Oh my god*, she thought, *he really is the most amazing man.* She sucked the thick chocolate ice cream through the straw so fast it collapsed on itself making them both laugh. Two hours of relaxing passed quickly and they were soon interrupted by the physical therapist and his assistant. He explained the series of exercises she would be doing four times per week and what each of them would do. He also gave Garrett a chart with all of them listed as well as an explanation of how to do each so that they would have a reference once she got home.

For the most part it was a lot of stretching along with some strength building using balance balls and resistance bands. She was familiar with almost all of it from dance workouts. She figured it would be no problem; she could just rely on muscle memory. It was a short consultation. Kaylie was pleasantly surprised when they told her she would have just one appointment with them while still admitted then they would check in with how she was doing from home. The one during her stay was mostly just going to be them supervising her to make sure that she was doing everything correctly. It was important to see that there were no issues with her injuries other than the expected aches and pains.

Once he said she could check in from home she got excited, exclaiming she would be free of doctors once they let her go. However her joy was doused quickly when he explained she would be checking in by coming in once a week to let them know how her home exercises were going. Disappointed but still grateful for the thought of her own bed she agreed.

When he left the shift nurse came in to check her vital signs and machine readouts. She smiled at Kaylie, who smiled back. The unexpected response threw the nurse off for a moment but she recovered quickly then wished Kaylie a good night. Just before she left she reminded Garrett that visiting hours were done in fifteen minutes. They spent the last couple minutes together talking about how Garrett would set up her dance workout area with the exercise chart and all the bands she would be using. He kissed her goodnight before heading home. Today was the first time she really felt like he was there for her.

She knew she still had a few more days to be kept in this horrible hospital bed but at least there was a light at the end of the tunnel. People were talking to her about going home. She leaned back and stretched her arms up over her head. Breathing deep she was delighted by the absence of stabbing pain. The surgery left a small incision mark and would take some healing but she felt so much better than she had previously it was hard to believe and she was grateful for that. As she stretched she became aware of a smell somewhere around her. She sniffed her blanket, checked the pillow but couldn't find the source.

Her oily hair slipped into her face and she realized that the smell was her. She had been prisoner to this bed for days and hadn't been able to shower. One more deep sniff confirmed what she really needed right now. She rang the call button. When the nurse came in she asked if they had anything that would help. She giggled and said she would get everything she could find.

Kaylie was astonished when she returned with a bucket full of supplies. She found a razor, shaving cream, toothbrush and toothpaste, dry shampoo, and a brush. She also found a couple towels and deodorant. She turned on the television while she opened everything. She asked the nurse to grab some water before she left. The next hour was a wonderment of cleanliness, and when she was done she stretched out and smiled the biggest smile she had in a long time. She dozed off feeling amazing. She slept deep and dreamless, smiling the entire night.

Chapter 13

Detective Meyar went home after talking to the Dentons to try to get some sleep. It was a long day and was quickly turning into a very long night indeed. He lay in bed, flipping through channels but not really seeing any of it. His mind was still on the homeless Nick Marks that had been the suspect in a robbery years ago, and the strong possibility he could be connected to both the young dancer and the recently deceased Justin Denton. He was sure there had to be a connection but no matter how hard he racked his brain he couldn't figure it out.

He went over and over the information in his head but it just kept coming up with blank spots he didn't seem to be able to fill in. Finally he got up and stumbled over to the desk in the corner. He pulled a notepad and pen from the top drawer and began writing everything out so he could more clearly see the questions he needed answered. He had to try to find exactly what he needed so he knew what he was looking for once he went in tomorrow and had access to the case files. The flow chart he created took less than an hour but he now clearly saw a great deal seemed to center around Kyle and Nick Marks. There was possibly some connection with Kyle's wife Sabrina as well. He wandered back to bed and eventually fell asleep, mind still racing.

Chapter 14

Kaylie woke up the next morning not surprised to find the sunny face of Cindy staring at her. She grabbed the notebook and threw it at the therapist.

"If you want to know what's going on, read this." She stated matter-of-factly. "You don't do anything other than make me feel terrible about myself then leave. All I have all day is the notebooks to tell my feelings to and it doesn't give me any ways of dealing with them."

"So you have been using the notebooks, great." She made a note in her chart and flipped through the pages without really reading anything. "I'm happy to see you have found them useful."

"Yeah, I use them so if you want to know what's going on then read those, otherwise disappear like you always do. It's all you know how to do." Kaylie turned on her side and closed her eyes.

"How are your ribs and lungs feeling after the surgery?" Kaylie turned back to face her.

"You actually want to talk about something real and important today?"

"Yes I'm curious how you're doing. I know that you had part of a rib pressing into the side of your lung. You must feel relieved to have that taken care of."

"Yeah, that is exactly how I feel."

"And how was your consultation for rehabilitation?"

"Can't we just call it PT?"

"Physical therapy then, fine, how did it go?"

"It was great, should be a breeze." She waved her hand dismissively for emphasis. "I'm used to all of the exercises from dance so it will be easy. Should be able to get back to my old self in no time."

"It will probably be difficult at first and you know that they mentioned some of the injuries may leave you with limitations."

"You are just determined to ruin each and every day for me, aren't you?"

"I am just pointing out the facts. I want to make sure you are being realistic."

"Whatever, I'm tired of this, I am going back to sleep." She turned back over and closed her eyes, willing sleep to take her again. After five minutes she gave up and turned back to face the impossibly patient woman still smiling at her.

"Well I can see we are not going to make much more progress today. I do however have a surprise for you." She got up and headed for the door. Oh god, Kaylie thought, another stupid breakfast game. Just then the door burst open and Cindy was nearly trampled as her mom and dad bombarded her with hugs and kisses. The site of her parent's faces made her cry instantly. Through the tears she saw Garrett leaning against the doorframe. She threw her arms around her mom's neck and hung on tight, ignoring the pain that shot through her body with the motion. She then gave her father the same treatment. This was amazing.

Cindy left during the hug exchange and Garrett took a seat on the far side of the room, smiling as he enjoyed the show. He listened and joined in the conversation from time to time. He was awed by the power of seeing the woman he loved moved so much by something as simple as a hug from her mother. It was the best part of the week and the first day he had seen her look truly happy. When Cindy mentioned the idea of having them come he had been skeptical but as soon as the notion was on the table her mom had practically yelled her agreement. She said they would start packing right away.

Coming from Lansing, Michigan they always took the train. It saved them from having to drive in Chicago traffic and was far cheaper than flying. Her father always refused to travel west of

88

Chicago which was one of the biggest reasons Kaylie accepted the dancing position there instead of one of the bigger companies on the west coast who also expressed interest in her. Now here they were sharing a day so filled with jubilation it was almost possible to forget it was in a hospital room.

They laughed and talked all day. Even some of the doctors that tried to come in and take her off for more updated tests were persuaded, upon seeing her, to reschedule for the next day. Everyone was just relieved to see her happy and more relaxed. It was a great day. Garrett practically had to physically remove her parents from the room to take them to get settled into their hotel. He had offered the second room at their apartment but they, as always, said they didn't want to be a burden and booked a hotel online.

Garrett loved Kaylie's mom, though they didn't look alike very much he still always believed that looking at her he could see what his wife would be like thirty years into marriage. It thrilled him. He was nothing like her father but still believed that they would be together forever just like these idols of hers. After dropping off their luggage he suggested dinner but following the train ride and the long day in the hospital they gently declined.

Garrett walked downstairs and hopped on the L, heading home. He leaned against the window as he watched the scenery pass from streets and traffic to buildings and back again. Getting off the train he stopped at the bottom of the platform to buy a paper to read once he got home. It was bitterly cold. He rushed through the wind into the warmth of the apartment. He kept his coat on while he opened a can of soup and got the stove going.

Even though it was getting late he still brewed up a pot of coffee. As it began percolating he tossed the paper on the table before heading off to change into something more comfortable. When he came back he was reaching for the coffee mugs when a headline caught his eye. *Shooting Victim Dies Days After Attack.* He

89

snatched up the paper and read the article closely. The man that had been shot the same night as Kaylie's accident had passed away at the hospital. The reporter went on to say the police were investigating the homicide and were in search of a connection between a robbery suspect from a previous crime and the two crimes from last week.

It wasn't until the soup began boiling over the side of the pan that he finally put the paper down. He walked over to the stove still rereading the article from a distance. He couldn't help but wonder about the previous robbery. There was also something nagging him about the name of the man that died, Justin Denton. Why did that name sound so familiar? He knew there was a reason he should know that name. His parents had requested very little personal information be put in about him so they could deal with the tragedy as a private family affair but he knew there was something there. Maybe Kaylie would know, he thought. He would have to ask her tomorrow.

Chapter 15

That same morning while Kaylie was hugging her mom and dad, Detective Meyar was pouring over case files. He looked at everything about Nick Marks and the interviews with his family. He seemed to have a very deep issue with Kyle and Sabrina's success. He had been a performer as a child and had, at one point attempted to become a part of the dance studio owned and operated by his sister-in-law. She said in her interview, though, that he had been very self-involved acting menacing toward the other performers. She was worried about the safety of the other dancers. He had even gotten into an argument with the musical director about the best way to highlight his abilities.

When he threatened her for not letting him into the company, Kyle stepped in and told him to get out and stay away from his family. He left but had destroyed several rooms in the house during the process. They had a gun stolen a month previous, it was the same caliber as the one used in the robbery but the time between the crimes kept him from being considered a suspect at the time. After the robbery they began looking for him and though he was eventually been brought in for questioning, they never found the gun or found anything conclusive to hold him on. All evidence against him had been very circumstantial and the DA never felt fully confident in bringing charges against him. Once he was released they continued the investigation but it had never been closed.

Nick had fallen off the grid after that. While the police knew he had been staying off and on at a shelter in Lincoln Park. If he was the man who caused the accident he hijacked the cab several miles away and the crash was alongside Garfield Park. They were heading toward the highway so the detectives were completely baffled as to where to start looking. He thought it best to start with the estranged family and try to fill in at least a few of the missing links.

Meyar called his partner. He asked him to pick up some coffee on the way into the office; it was going to be a very long day. He knew he would have to go talk to Kyle and Sabrina. Once he learned what he could from them he was also going to have to go talk to Kaylie. He knew she would be able to fill in some of the blanks as well, at least he hoped she would. He called Kyle Marks to make sure he would be home and asked if his wife was available to speak with him as well. Kyle told him he would make sure she was but cautioned that she was quite upset right now. She was feeling overwhelmed by everything going on.

Detective Meyar said he understood making a mental note to do his best to keep her part short if possible. He was already outside waiting when his partner arrived. He greedily took the coffee, gulping down half of the cup without regard to the temperature then snatched his keys out of his pocket, leading the way to the car. They didn't speak on the ride. Instead Meyar handed over the file along with his notes to review while he drove. John had been involved with the original investigation into Nick Marks so a lot of the information was just a refresher for him. By the time they reached the Marks' residence they felt fully prepared to go in and try to get the rest of the big picture.

Sabrina opened the door before the two detectives reached the porch and welcomed them in with a sweeping motion toward the living room. Their house was warm with cherry hardwood floors and bold red accent walls broken only by a white chair rail. It was tastefully decorated and while they took seats on the edge of the sofa to wait, she adjusted a painting then flopped into the easy chair facing them.

"How can we help you Detective?" She asked, not bothering to wait for her husband to join them. They shifted and looked at one another. Finally Meyar cleared his throat, jumping right in.

"Well ma'am, we wanted to talk to your husband about his brother Nick."

"Why?" Her face pinched at the mention of her brother-in-law. "Will Mr. Marks be joining us?"

"Yeah." She waved a hand dismissively toward the kitchen then continued. "He'll be here in a minute or two. Why do you want to talk about Nick?"

"Well, as you know he had been a suspect in a robbery a couple years ago."

"I remember, he was an asshole and got an attitude at my studio. We kicked him out."

"Right, and you had also reported your husband's gun stolen a month before you asked him to leave."

"Yeah, he stole it. You thought he used it in the robbery but if I remember the shot didn't kill anyone."

"Correct, but the gun was used. At least one of the same make and caliber was used and it was never recovered. Assuming your brother-in-law was the one that committed the crime, he shot the man in the shoulder and again shot into the wall leaving a bullet for comparison. We brought him in for questioning but could never make a case strong enough to hold him."

"So, again, why do you want to talk about him? Did he do something else now?"

"We would just like to find him to talk to him. He is a person of interest at this time."

She sat up a little and narrowed her eyes. Looking back and forth between the two, suspicion written across her face. "Did he have something to do with Justin?"

Detective Meyar was taken aback. "Justin, ma'am?"

"First of all, stop calling me ma'am, I am not that old. Second, Justin Denton, he was my musical director. He was attacked the other night and just died from his injuries."

"Mr. Denton worked for you as well?"

"Yes he worked for me," she snapped. Then, more quietly, "What do you mean as well?"

"Do you have a dancer by the name of Akaylia Reynolds?"

"Kaylie," Sabrina immediately corrected him, just as Kaylie herself had done. "Yes, she dances for my company." There was a short pause as her eyes widened. Tears welled up immediately "Oh my god!" She screamed as she broke down crying. Meyar was already writing in his notepad. John was scanning the information in Nick's file again. He noticed something; the previous victim had also worked for the dance company.

Just then, Kyle came in and saw his wife curled up in a little ball on the chair, sobbing. He looked accusingly at the two officers sitting on the other side of the room. Meyar began to get to his feet and shake Kyle's hand but he stopped him by turning his back to attend to Sabrina. Once he was sure she would be all right for a moment he turned his attention back to the two men. He strode across the room and gave each a short obligatory handshake before taking a seat in the chair next to Sabrina.

"What can I do for you gentlemen?" Kyle asked rubbing Sabrina's leg, letting her know he was there.

"Mr. Marks, we had hoped to learn anything you might know about your brother's whereabouts."

"Why are you looking for Nick?" He glanced at the sobbing heap next to him, wondering how his useless brother could be connected to her clear frustration.

"We believe he was involved in the attack last weekend."

"The attack? You mean the murder of Justin?" Now it was starting to make sense. Justin had worked for Sabrina for years. He had stood strong with her against Nick when he had tried to force his way into the company. "You think Nick killed Justin?"

"We believe the gun used was the one you reported stolen years ago just before you kicked him out. It was the same one used in the robbery right after that incident. We had talked to him back then

94

but we never found the gun." John shifted uncomfortably. They had already had this conversation four years ago. Now he felt like they were starting over at square one again.

"I remember. The last victim was connected with her company as well. So what, you think he is targeting Sabrina and her dance staff?" He was puzzled, if Nick really was still holding a grudge, why would he have stayed away for the past three years?

"Do you have any idea where he may be, or have you had any contact with him recently?"

"The last time I saw him was when you all released him. He came pounding on our door but we told him he wasn't welcome anywhere near our family ever again."

"Do you have any other family or friends that might have taken him in?"

"No. I heard that he was staying in a shelter at one point but never cared enough to go and see. I no longer consider him family."

"I understand. We also have information about the shelter but when we contacted them, the director told us he hadn't been there for a couple years. He was asked to leave after causing an altercation with another man during dinner."

"That doesn't surprise me. So you want to talk to him about killing Justin?" He turned to Sabrina who had finally gotten herself under control. She was sitting up beside him.

"It isn't just Justin honey."

"What do you mean? What else did he do?"

"Its Kaylie babe, they think he was the bastard that hijacked her cab." Tears started trickling down her cheeks again but she kept it mostly under control. "He is getting back at me by going after people close to me."

"Sabrina, why would he have stopped for nearly three years and then go after these people now?"

"Who knows what he was doing for the last couple years. He's crazy." She got quiet as another thought dawned on her. "The song he tried to perform to is opening the summer show."

"What show?" Detective Meyar looked up from his notes.

"Our summer recital. It has various numbers and the song he insisted was his is the solo opening the show. When he came in and demanded to become a part of our company he tried to perform it but his attempt was a joke. Justin used an acoustic version of the song and Nick lost it screaming that the music threw him off. He went on a rant stating he was the best dancer that had ever walked through the door."

"Ok, I understand that he might go after Justin although it wasn't his fault. But why wait so long? And why go after Kaylie? She wasn't even part of the company three years ago." Sabrina shook her head. She couldn't explain why he had waited but the reason for targeting her seemed all too obvious to Sabrina, she was performing the number he had auditioned.

"We released the promo stuff for the show. It shows Kaylie and says she is performing the solo, the one that he considered his." She rubbed away the tears that threatened to overtake her again. "I don't think the attack was random, he went after her because of the solo."

The officers had been listening intently to the exchange. With a motive becoming clear they only had one question left. Clearing his throat to bring focus back to him Meyar asked, "How could he possibly have known either would be there though?"

"Well Justin still has a landline, he could have looked up the address online. The poor dear was only a block away from home so he could have just followed him. For Kaylie though I don't know. I did talk to Garrett about them going out to dinner during the day but it was over the phone. I have no idea how he could have heard." She thought about it for a while. "All I can suggest is that you talk to Garrett and see what he has to say."

"Do you by chance have a picture of Nick? I want to show it to Miss Reynolds and see if she recognizes him."

"I have a couple I'm sure but they are from years ago. With him living on the street I am sure he would look completely different."

"Anything you have would be great; since we never officially arrested him we do not have any mug shots of him." Sabrina left the room to retrieve a photo album. She came back flipping through the pages until she found the picture she had been searching for. She nearly tore the protective covering when opening it to pull out the photograph. She tossed it into the waiting hands of the detectives and closed the book sitting it on the side table next to her without looking.

She kept her eyes trained on Meyar as he examined the picture. He compared it to something in his notebook. John peered over his shoulder and gave a slight shudder at the reminder of the odd man he had interviewed years ago. There was something off about him. The creepy feeling he left had never completely gone away. He settled back while Meyar finished reading the suspect description.

Meyar was convinced now, even more than he had been before; this was the man that had killed Justin Denton and had nearly killed Akaylia Reynolds. He checked his watch. It was already nearing noon. He really wanted to go to the hospital to speak with Kaylie and Garrett before it got too late and she fell asleep from her medications. He stood up and thanked Kyle and Sabrina Marks promising to keep in touch with updates. As they strode down the front hallway he could hear the hurried whispering and beginnings of sobbing again.

The detectives rushed to their car. Meyar already had the car in gear before the doors were closed. They needed to get to Kaylie to fill in the rest of the blanks as well as find out any further information she and Garrett may know. They discussed how Nick could have possibly known about them going to the restaurant that night but until they spoke with Garrett they knew it would all be speculation. It only took twelve minutes for the two officers to reach the hospital but it felt like an eternity. They parked the car in the first available space then using all of their control to keep from running all the way to the room they went inside to speak to Kaylie.

John stopped by the nurse's station to confirm she was in her room then caught back up to Meyar, nodding that she was inside. Meyar pushed through the door without knocking and stumbled into a silent room filled with nothing but the sound of a pen scratching across paper. Kaylie was so intent on what she was writing even the sound of the officers crashing into the room didn't faze her. She was almost in a trance as she scribbled her experiences and anticipation for the upcoming physical therapy. She was feeling confident. She had decided the doctors were wrong; she would dance again. She also knew she would be in the summer concert and right then she felt nothing could bring her down.

Detective Meyar cleared his throat but she took no notice of him. He tried again but she simply flipped the page in her notebook and continued to write. "Excuse me," he tried. Still nothing. "Miss Reynolds, I really need to talk to you."

"Kaylie." She automatically corrected as she finished the thought she had been putting down. Closing the notebook slowly she placed it aside, calmly looking at the officers. "What can I do for you detective?"

"I was wondering if you recognize any of these men." He handed her a card with six photographs on it including the picture provided of Nick Marks. Before she even looked at it she examined him.

"How is your investigation going?" She was holding the picture card but kept her eyes trained on him. He waited patiently for her to look at the pictures. He needed to know for sure.

"We are still moving forward. It would help very much if you would look at the photos and let me know if you recognize anyone." Kaylie looked past him, over his right shoulder and waved. Meyar felt someone push past him as Garrett entered behind him taking a seat on the bed beside her. Meyar sighed and pulled up a chair at the foot of the bed.

"Detective, how are you?" Garrett asked as he handed Kaylie a cup of water.

"We're here hoping that Kaylie can identify one of the men on the card I gave her. We have gotten some information to share with you and of course, some more questions to ask but first and foremost is the picture." Garrett glanced down at the card in her hand then looked her in the eye.

"Don't worry, I'm going to be right here honey. Just take your time and look closely at the pictures. If you see someone just squeeze my hand." She laced her fingers through his and raised the card, finally tearing her gaze away from the officer to fix it on the first photo on the card. She touched on each of the three that made up the top row but nothing jumped out at her. She took a deep breath then lowered her eyes to the three on the bottom row. The first picture was all it took, tears jumped to her eyes and she screamed as she squeezed Garrett's hand.

"It's him, oh my god, it's him!" She collapsed into his arms and lost herself in the sobs. She was shaking. He held her, rubbing her shoulders. He helped her back against the pillows where she curled up into a ball. The stretching of her spine when curling up cut straight through the numbing of the painkillers and she screamed again. He watched helplessly as she shuddered and buried her face under the pillow. He grasped her hand and returned focus to the detectives.

"What the hell was that?" He snapped angrily. "You could have warned her or at least led into it so she was slightly prepared. Who the hell is it anyway?"

"I am sorry but we couldn't give anything away just in case she didn't recognize anyone. We still need her to say for sure who it is that she recognizes and if she knows his name." He looked at her doubtfully knowing that her talking wasn't likely anytime soon. "We now know she was able to pick out the man that attacked her and unfortunately we still need to ask her a couple questions about him. But we also would like to get a little information from you if possible."

"What do you need from me?"

"The man that hijacked your fiancé's cab may have targeted her. We believe he may have been waiting outside the restaurant. It's possible he was just waiting for a time when she was alone. Is there any way that someone could have known where the two of you were going to dinner that night?"

"I don't think so," he started. "I was sending out some of the promo materials for the show most of the day." He stopped, thinking back to the events of that day. "I put up one of the posters myself as sort of a celebration for Kaylie and her solo at the library."

"Sabrina mentioned that you and she and discussed your dinner plans on the phone."

"Oh yeah, I called her after the poster was up to let her know how it looked and when she mentioned that she was going to give Kaylie the news right before she left I told her that I was going to take her out for dinner at Café Le Amile." He stopped, eyes widening. "Are you telling me that I did this to her? Some crazy guy heard me say the name and showed up to hurt her? I don't understand, why would anyone target her? She has never done anything to anyone in her life."

"The man we believe is responsible for the attack is actually the estranged brother-in-law of Sabrina Marks."

"What?" he cried out, incredulously.

"What?" Came the meek question, startling both men. They turned to the tear stained Kaylie as she sat up and sniffled. "Sabrina knows that man?"

100

"Kaylie," Detective Meyar tried to sound soothing. His hands swung at his sides, unsure suddenly of what they should be doing. He took a deep breath, doing his best to soften his features as he spoke. "Sabrina's husband Kyle has a brother named Nick. We have strong reason to believe he is the man that you recognized. Can you please point out the picture so I know for sure it is the same man?"

She snatched up the hateful picture card and pointed to the bottom left corner so hard she nearly put her finger through the photo. "That's him, that's the bastard that tried to kill me. He also said he killed someone else that night, but you said you were going to look into that." She looked at him with her puffy, red-rimmed eyes and waited for his answer.

"He did rob another man and beat him severely. He was brought here in a coma but unfortunately he didn't make it. I'm very sorry."

"That's terrible." She grew quiet for a moment. "Why are you apologizing to me? I didn't know the man." Her eyes narrowed on the detective. "Or did I?" Fresh tears were threatening to spill over and though he knew his news would not be welcome, he wanted her to know.

"The robbery victim was a man named Justin Denton, Kaylie. He was the musical director for your dance company."

"Oh God," she whispered. The flood began once more. She fought it for a moment, using her fists to scrub at her cheeks. When they wouldn't stop she resigned herself to her tears.

"So you think he knew I was taking her out to dinner and after he killed the musical director he came all the way to the restaurant to try and hurt Kaylie?"

"Mr. Denton lived just a couple blocks from the restaurant. We believe that yes, he heard your conversation with Mrs. Marks and targeted Ms. Reynolds and Mr. Denton after seeing the promotional material for the show. Mrs. Marks told us her brother-in-law fancies himself a performer and auditioned several years ago to the same music that inspired the show Kaylie was supposed to be performing in. He selected the same number that inspired her solo piece from what Mrs. Marks has told us. We are doing everything we can to find him as quickly as possible."

"You aren't doing enough." She wailed through her tears. Garrett had temporarily given up trying to comfort her and was glaring across the room at Detective Meyar and the recently joined Detective John Rommel.

"You are unbelievable," he whispered. "You dare to come in here and without warning you throw this tragedy in her face. Then tell her that not only was it not random but a good friend she didn't even know was hurt, was actually killed by the same man."

"I understand that this is a difficult time but we just..."

"You don't understand anything," Garrett said through gritted teeth. Standing slowly he regarded the officers. "Get the hell away from her, from us. Do not come back unless you have caught the monster that did this and if you try to come near her again I promise you it will be something you regret."

Meyar chose not to point out that threatening an officer was not a great idea. This was obviously a terribly stressful time and the young man was just trying to protect her from the pain he couldn't take away. The officers departed reluctantly, stopping to ask the nurse to check in on them in a little while. They left and headed back to the office. A few of the blanks had been filled in. Though it had driven Kaylie to tears, Meyar still felt it had been a productive day.

Chapter 16

"Kaylie, honey?" Garrett was rubbing her back, trying to get her calmed down. She hadn't responded for almost an hour. She finally stopped crying about fifteen minutes ago but now she was just lying on her side staring at the wall. He tried to turn her head so he could see her eyes but the dead blank stare was more than he could handle. "I'm going to go grab something to eat baby, do you want anything?" He waited, listening to the sound of her breathing. When she continued to simply stare he got to his feet. "I'll be back before the end of visiting hours."

She didn't respond. The blank stare continued as he quietly walked out, watching her the entire time until the door clicked closed. The cafeteria was scarce. He grabbed a small salad and a large soda. Eating quickly it didn't take long for him to finish. He didn't taste any of the food, he just wanted to get back and spend as much time with her as possible. Still it was difficult to make himself get up. He had no idea how to make her feel better.

He sat at the table staring at his hands, wishing he had answers to questions he wasn't even sure of. She was so lost. He felt exactly the same way sitting at her side. He fiddled with the straw in his soda, nearly dumping the cup when his phone vibrated on the tray. He looked at the caller ID. It was Kaylie's parents. He toyed with the idea of letting it go to voicemail but finally answered it on the last ring.

"Hello?" His voice was rough. He cleared his throat and tried again. "Hello?"

"Garrett, I'm so glad I caught you son. We tried calling Kaylie's room but there isn't any answer. I didn't think she was scheduled for any tests this late. Is everything ok?" Her father's anxious voice came through in a rush.

103

"Kaylie is there but she is having a hard time. The detectives came in to speak with her and she found out the person they think could be responsible for her accident. Apparently it's the brother-in-law of her company founder Sabrina." Garrett rubbed his eyes and pinched the bridge of his nose trying to force back an impending headache. "She will be ok."

"Garrett, where are you? Why didn't you answer the phone in her room?"

"I am down in the cafeteria. After the detectives left she just stared at the wall. She wouldn't talk to me. I wanted to give her some space to process what we learned so I came down here to grab a bite."

"Please go check on her again. She doesn't handle stress well, outside of the pressures of performing of course. I know it is difficult but please just go see how she is doing." He paused. Garrett could hear him relaying all the information to Kaylie's mom. When he came back on the phone there was a sense of fatigue behind his words. "Would it be better if we came to visit her ourselves tonight?"

"No, I will go see how she is doing. I can call you when I leave and we can all come up tomorrow if you like. I don't want to overwhelm her."

They said their goodbyes and Garrett threw away his trash. Something about the way her dad mentioned she didn't handle anxiety well was gnawing at him. He ran to the elevator but decided he didn't have the patience so he found the nearest stairwell and climbed them two at a time all the way to the fifth floor.

When he pushed through the door of her room he startled the nurse doing her customary nightly check. Her expression was grim as she checked Kaylie's blood pressure machine readout. She gazed at Garrett then back at Kaylie shaking her head. She gathered everything up and scooted around Garrett, exiting without a word.

He slowly made his way over to her and sat at the edge of the bed. For a moment he just watched her. She was still lying exactly as she had been. He tried to hold her hand but it was limp. He squeezed a few times but let go when she didn't grasp his back. He settled for rubbing her back again, just being there for her. "Kaylie, I know this is hard but it really is going to be ok."

He still got no response from her. She was just there, like a life sized sad doll. The last forty-five minutes of visiting hours was spent in silence. When the nurse came in to let him know she once again looked at Kaylie and left shaking her head. "I have to go Kaylie," he leaned down and kissed her on the forehead. "I love you, your parents want to come in and see you tomorrow. I hope you're feeling better then, honey."

She lay there staring at the wall. She hadn't moved since she stopped crying, hadn't eaten or spoken. As he left the room he told the nurse on duty what her parent said about her stress. He asked them to check on her more frequently through the night and notify him if anything changed. They agreed and made a note.

An hour or so after Garrett went home the woman at the desk saw the request. The nurse went in and saw Kaylie was still on her side facing the wall. She mistakenly thought that Kaylie had fallen asleep and closed the door. Kaylie didn't sleep that night at all. When one of the nurses came in around midnight to check the machines, her cold dead stare nearly made her scream. She noted everything quickly in the medical chart then left swearing she wouldn't go back in that night unless she had too. The look on Kaylie's face had scared her to her core.

Chapter 17

The next morning Cindy came in and sat down as usual but was not met with the normal sarcasm or even the unusual cooperation she sometimes encountered. "Good morning."

The sunny greeting got no response. Cindy stood up and checked to see that Kaylie was indeed awake. The look on her face sent a chill down Cindy's spine. There was no emotion, just a blank stare. She tried again with no response at all. Cindy began noting the incident in the chart. This normally was met with a comment but today it got nothing, not even a sigh.

The nurse came into the silent room, startling the therapist. She checked Kaylie and asked about breakfast but got nothing. She asked to speak with Cindy out in the hall. As the women left it never occurred to either that Kaylie was so far gone she wouldn't have heard them anyway.

"I think something may be very wrong. She has been like that since yesterday afternoon. She didn't eat dinner. She hasn't had breakfast. If this continues we will have to start feeding her through the IV." The nurse was wringing her hands as she peeked at the door.

"Well make sure she gets the nutrition she needs. What happened? Do you know why she dropped into this state?" Cindy herself looked back over her shoulder at the door.

"I don't know what happened. I wasn't here yesterday but I will ask to see if anyone else any ideas." Still wringing her hands, she scurried off down the hall. Cindy watched her go then walked back into the room.

"Kaylie?" She walked a couple of feet and tried again. "Kaylie? I can see something is bothering you. The nurse tells me you have been quiet since yesterday. What happened Kaylie?" No movement, no response. Cindy inched her way over to the bed crouching in front of Kaylie trying to look her in the eye. "I need to know what happened yesterday. Why aren't you talking or eating?"

The blank stare went on. There was no focal point; she was just staring into space. Seeing nothing, hearing nothing. She was lost within her own head. Cindy sat with her and tried to hold her hand for a while but Kaylie never said a word the entire hour. She was breathing, there was an occasional blink of her eyes but those were the only signs of life. Cindy slowly walked around the side of the bed and picked up her belongings. This was a terrible sight. What was worse was she had no idea how to begin helping when she wasn't sure how it started.

She backed up to the door and let out a long, sad sigh. "I'm going to help you Kaylie," she promised. "I don't know what happened but we are going to get you through this."

She hung her head and exited the still silent room. She slipped on her jacket and turned almost running into Garrett. His eyes were bloodshot from lack of sleep. His shoulders hung beneath the tremendous weight he was so obviously carrying. She leaned against the wall and gave him a weak smile. "How are you doing Garrett?"

He struggled to lift his head up and meet her gaze. She saw the corners of his mouth twitch but a smile was beyond him today. He settled for a half-hearted shrug. He nodded his head toward the door. "How is she?"

"I don't know."

"What does that mean?"

"She won't move or talk. The nurses tell me she hasn't eaten. She just lays there and stares at nothing."

"Still? Shit, I wanted to come by and check on her to see how she was doing before I brought her parents over from the hotel."

"I really would recommend against them seeing her like this."
She thought for a minute. "What do you mean still? When did this
start?"

"Yesterday, mid-afternoon. The detective and, I assume his
partner, stopped by and without warning showed her a picture of
the guy that did this to her."

"They know who it is? They just showed her a picture of him?"

"They gave her what they called a photo array. On it was a
picture of the guy that had hijacked her cab. She was hysterical.
Then, just when she started to get herself under control again, they
told her even more bad news."

"What did they tell her?"

"They have apparently figured out that the guy that jumped her
taxi is related to Sabrina and her husband. They think she was
targeted because of dancing for Sabrina. Not only did that bastard
take her dream away from her, he did it because of the dancing
itself. They also told her that the musical director for the company
was attacked the same night and had died. She is completely
devastated."

"I can only imagine. She was in no condition to deal with that.
She was only starting to accept her injuries, not even the long term
ramifications of what she's gone through." Cindy closed her eyes
and let out a long breath as she leaned her head back tapping it on
the wall, thinking. She fished a card out of her briefcase and
handed it to Garrett. "I would strongly suggest that you keep her
parents away for today and please, when she does come out of this,
give me a call. I will continue to check in on her every morning."

Garrett watched her wander on down the hall. Usually she was so
enthusiastic that she practically bounced as she walked. Today,
however, trudging seemed a far more appropriate description. She
looked like she was now carrying the same weight that Garrett
himself was holding. He watched her until she disappeared around
the corner then turned back to Kaylie's room. Even the door in

front of him seemed to give a sigh; he reached out and gripped the handle but didn't turn it.

He so longed to go in and hold Kaylie, to hold his fiancé, and comfort her for the pain she had had to endure yesterday. But the girl lying in there wasn't the woman he loved. She was just the shell right now. He had to believe she would come through this the same way she had gotten past the diagnosis. He wanted to believe that the stubborn strength inside her would prevail, but the look on her face yesterday was haunting. He didn't feel he had the strength to deal with it today. He let his arm drop while turning away.

As he walked back out to the street he did his best to think of what he was going to tell her parents about why they couldn't go see their daughter. Her mother was so close with her and as much pain as Kaylie was in; he knew it would kill her mother to have to see her that way. Her father was the strong silent type most of the time but seeing his baby girl in that hospital bed had definitely put a couple of cracks in his tough exterior. The ride to the hotel was short. Garrett was still trying to figure out the right excuse when he walked into the lobby.

Shaking off the snow that had packed around his ankles during the walk from the station he looked up and saw that her parents were sitting on one of the lounge sets waiting for him. Her mother grabbed her purse and stood up as soon as she saw him, the smile beaming on her face warm enough to melt the winter itself. She tugged at her husband's shoulder to get him to his feet faster but he didn't hurry. Unlike his wife, he had already read the expression on Garrett's face. He knew he was not going to be seeing his daughter today.

They had travelled for hours on that train and tomorrow morning they would board it again and head back home. He knew they were going to do so without the chance to spend any more time with Kaylie. Her mom kept tugging until he slapped her hand away. He gently turned her back toward their future son-in-law and she finally saw his face. He knew he hadn't hidden the frustration but was hoping that he would be able to keep the reason from them. He brightened as much as he could. "How are you doing this morning?"

"What is going on with Akaylia, Garrett?" Her dad was always so direct. Garrett fumbled for a moment gathering his thoughts and hoping they came out with some confidence.

"I just came from the hospital. They are going to have her in consultations and tests all day so unfortunately we can't go. I am sorry you came all the way here for nothing."

"It wasn't for nothing, Garrett," he replied calmly. He squeezed his wife's shoulder and looked back at the young man in front of him. He didn't believe a word that had just been told to him but for the sake of her mother he was going to go along with it. Garrett saw all of this and gave a slight smile as a form of thank you. "We saw her. If this is what she needs to get better then we understand and wouldn't want to interrupt any treatment."

"So we won't be able to see her at all today?" Her mother asked, the smile finally fading and reality settling in. "Well that is just plain impolite."

Garrett and her father both broke into laughter. It was such a tense and frustrating situation. They all were scared for her but here was her mother, mad at the doctors for scheduling tests and consultations, so she thought, while they were visiting and therefore taking time away from them. It was just the perfect comment to lighten the mood. Once he had gotten himself under control, Garrett suggested lunch and a walk along Michigan Ave.

He remembered how much Kaylie had loved walking up and down there when she first moved here. She even still made it a point to go for one or two of her runs each week along the waterfront, usually stopping by either Buckingham Fountain or Millennium Park on her way to Navy Pier. It was now and always had been her favorite place in the entire city. Her parents knew this too. They had vacationed here once when she was a child and had taken her to the top of Sears Tower but the draw of the water had found her even then/ She spent more time looking out at Lake Michigan than almost anything else they did that trip.

Her mom mentioned this several times during their walk. When they found a little café a block away from the park she insisted they stop for lunch. It was a pleasant afternoon and Garrett was glad to get to spend it with them, but in the back of his mind he kept thinking about Cindy's observations and the fact that the nurses said Kaylie hadn't been eating. She had slipped so far back from the news yesterday that if her recovery got delayed or worse he wasn't sure she would be able to handle it.

After finishing the walk and getting her parents back to their hotel he told them he needed to go home and finish a few things for work. He promised he would check on her later and call them tonight. Her father gave a sad though approving nod then led her mother back into the lobby. As soon as they were out of sight he took off running toward the train. He needed to get back and see her, hoping against hope that she was talking and eating again.

He took a seat and closed his eyes, massaging his temples. His head didn't hurt but the fatigue and frustration seemed to be relieved with the same motion. Taking a few deep breaths he tried to picture Kaylie as she had been yesterday morning before the officers descended to destroy her. He saw her smiling and nibbling on bacon. He saw them holding hands and talking. His smile was becoming less work until the picture in his head morphed into the memory of her curled into a ball and the detectives systematically annihilating her spirit. He felt the ice building up in his veins as his anger toward the police resurfaced.

The ride was no longer than it had ever been, but it seemed to be taking forever. He was so anxious to get that picture out of his mind it distracted him. When he jumped off the train he immediately slipped on ice, going down hard. A woman held out her hand and helped him up but before she could even ask if he was all right, he was already back on his feet and thanking her. As soon as he was sure he was steady he took off again and tore down the stairs. He was hopping down two at a time but kept a firm grasp on the handrail making sure he didn't take another tumble.

The nurses saw him coming, giving him a smile but the sorrow in their eyes gave away the truth. He slowed and eventually stopped, catching his breath as his body realized he wasn't going to take off again anytime soon. He leaned against the counter and gulped air until his heart slowed down, relaxing his muscles while stopping the pounding in his ears. The nurses watched him with a mix of awe and concern.

"Please tell me she is doing better." He gasped.

"I am sorry sir but she hasn't moved or spoken yet. We tried to get her to eat but so far she hasn't even looked at anything we brought in. She just lies there and stares. If this doesn't change soon it will begin to reverse her healing. We started feeding her intravenously but she needs movement."

"Can I see her and try to talk to her?"

"Yes sir, we all wish you luck, we know what you have both been going through." She was genuinely hoping he would get through to her. He walked into the blackness of the room. He felt along the wall until he found a switch for the light. He flicked the switch and screamed as her dead eyes confronted him. The doctors and nurses must have sat her up, he thought, when trying to get her to eat. So now she was staring into nothingness in full view instead of staring at the wall. It was creepy. The pale drawn skin of her face made his whole body prickle.

He walked around the side of the bed but her gaze remained fixed on nothing in front of her. He wanted to shake her, to snap her out of this, but he had no idea how she would react, assuming she reacted at all. Most important he didn't want to irritate the injuries. "Kaylie, baby, can you hear me?"

Nothing. "Kaylie, you have to start eating honey. The doctors say it can cause your healing to stop or even go backward. You don't want that, I know you want to get better." He was pleading. He could hear the desperation in his voice but he pressed on anyway. "Don't let him win, Kaylie. That man is a monster. What he did is unforgivable, but you survived because you are stronger than he is. Come on Kaylie, look at me."

He felt the tears coming from his complete exhaustion and the fear that he was losing her. He put his head down and rubbed his eyes. His felt himself losing faith and it broke his heart. He looked up at her and jumped when he saw she had turned her head. Though she was more looking through him than at him, it was still movement. His heart leapt. Her haunted stare was breaking him but fighting the despair was the little voice whispering hope that he could get through to her.

He took her hand and squeezed it tight. "Kaylie, please look at me, I know you can hear me, please look at me." He watched but there was no change in her expression. "Come on Kaylie, I know it's hard. I know it hurts but you are stronger than this. Don't let him win." His hands still tight on hers he watched and waited.

After what seemed like an hour he felt something land on his hand. He looked and saw a single bead of water. Looking up he saw tears streaming down her cheeks. There was focus in her eyes and the tears proved to him that he had broken through. He stood up and slid onto the bed with her putting his arms around her shoulders and though she was still looking at where he had been she was crying fully now and the shaking of her body came with an accompaniment of sounds. The gasping and sniffling were mostly muffled as she buried her face in his shoulder but the wails were loud enough that the door cracked open and a curious nurse poked her head in to verify that she really was hearing noise from the previously silent room.

113

Garrett glanced at her with his eyes only; he didn't dare move his head or anything else fearing it would startle her. She left, closing the door quietly and strolled back to the main station nodding to the other staff letting them know that yes, there had been a breakthrough. With any luck she would be talking and eating again soon.

Kaylie cried for a solid twenty minutes before finally sniffling herself dry. "I'm hungry," she mumbled into his shoulder. He laughed out loud and hugged her tight. She winced. He dropped his arms, afraid he'd hurt her, but it was just her head hurting from all the crying.

"What do you want honey? I will go and grab you anything." He stood up prepared to leave. Ready go to any restaurant he needed to.

"I really want a bagel and cream cheese."

"Sure." His smile was huge. "Let me go grab it for you baby, I will be right back." He ran from the room right into the poor candy striper that was walking past. He caught her but before she could say anything he was off and running again.

"Sir, where are you going?" The nurse called after him. He spun around and ran up to the counter smiling ear to ear.

"She's hungry, she wants a bagel, and I have to go get her a bagel." He checked the clock on the wall and an idea came to mind. "I know that visiting hours will be done soon but is there any way that I can go get her parents so they can say goodbye before they go back to Michigan tomorrow?"

She smiled and nodded. With everything that had been going on she couldn't even begin to imagine how her parents must feel. She was not going to deny them the chance to see their daughter one more time. She had barely gotten through her small stack of paperwork when the quiet hall was filled with hurried footsteps. She looked down the hall to see Garrett returning with two older people she only assumed were Kaylie's parents. The woman held a

114

bag from The Bagel Brothers and the excitement in their steps was mirrored in their expressions. She was gripping the bag so tightly her knuckles were white.

Garrett gave a little wave as they slipped by into Kaylie's room. Even through the closed door she could hear the delighted squeal as Kaylie and her mother saw each other. Glancing back over her shoulder at the clock she saw it was already quarter after nine but tonight visiting hours weren't going to end until the visitors decided for room 5341. She smiled to herself as she finished the papers and went to check on a few other patients.

Kaylie hugged her mom tight and held on. The past twenty-four hours were a complete blur but she intended to remember this. Her dad waited patiently and once it was his turn, he leaned down and kissed her forehead, giving a sweet gentle hug. She looked up, seeing the slight redness in his eyes and realized he had been crying. She'd only ever seen him cry twice before. She felt oddly surprised but very touched that this third time had been over her.

"How were your tests today honey?" Her mom asked. Garrett looked over her shoulder at Kaylie with wide eyes. He hadn't told her about the lie he felt forced to give her parents. He knew things were about to get awkward. She caught his eye and gave a confused look but there was an understanding between them. She smiled and looked back at her mom.

"I have been kind of out of it from all the medicine, mom. I honestly don't remember much about them." Garrett smiled a thank you to her then turned back to his conversation with her dad. "Do I smell bagels?"

"Yeah, Garrett said that you were craving them so we stopped on the way to pick some up for you." Kaylie tried to keep herself under control but she was ravenous. Once the bagel had its cream cheese on she tore it apart. Her mother smiled, watching as she went for a second bagel even eyeing a third.

The men talked in the corner enjoying the site of the women while just making small talk. The girls talked about wedding plans and when she was coming home in a month or so for her final dress fitting. The men talked about sports and the possibility that the Detroit Redwings would go to the playoffs yet again this year. Everyone was very careful to avoid the subject of dancing as well as what Kaylie would do once she was released and healed as much as she was expected to.

It was nearly midnight when, with a full stomach and the comfort of having her parents there, Kaylie yawned. Her mother, who had been fighting the fatigue herself took the sign. Standing up while gathering her coat and her husband she hugged Kaylie again. Her dad gave her another quick and hug, promising they would be in touch. He told her they hoped she would be back on her feet soon.

Garrett kissed her long and deep before heading out to take them back to the hotel then home to get some sleep himself. She let her body sink into the pillow and yawned again. She knew she had been awake for well over twenty-four hours but because she had been in such a deep trance she also felt like she had been sleeping. She turned on the television but didn't pay much attention to the infomercial that jumped on the screen. She just wanted the background noise. She closed her eyes as she laid the bed back into a nearly flat position.

She smiled at the memory of seeing her mom bursting into the room but just as quickly her smile turned to tears as she thought about Justin. He had been killed by the crazy, smelly man that had then tried to kill her. Sabrina knew him, was related to him even. He had wanted to kill her, not because she was in the cab but because he was after her.

She started to cry again as she thought about the poor driver. He had been killed because he wanted to stop and get away from the madman that was after her. She was the reason that the innocent driver had been killed. Guilt swept over her. The tears poured

116

down. She only sobbed for a few moments though, not because she got over it but because her mind and body finally agreed and gave out sending her into a troubled but deep sleep.

Chapter 18

The sun came in through the window as Kaylie woke up the next morning. She rolled her head stretching her neck. Before she opened her eyes, she turned her head to the left and slowly cracked her eyelids taking in the concerned face of the therapist she was beginning to despise. She sighed audibly while she rubbed the remaining sleep from her eyes.

"I don't have the patience for you today. I will write about it later if you want but please, no games today, I can't handle it."

"I'm just concerned about how you're doing. Garrett told me about the detectives coming and what they did."

"So you understand why I don't want to deal with any shit this morning."

"I just want to make sure that you aren't feeling guilty after finding out that the man was after you. It doesn't make you responsible for anything. It was all him and the police are going to bring him to justice, okay?"

"Yeah, sure, fine, whatever. Please just go away, leave me alone."

"We need to talk about this Kaylie." She stayed calm; this was going to be a battle. "You were so distressed you slipped into a sort of trance. It took more than a day to snap you back out of it. That is very serious."

"If you say so."

"Kaylie, tell me what happened." She watched carefully knowing that when she broke through it was going to be emotional. She didn't have to wait long; Kaylie snapped her head around and looked at her with slits of eyes.

"Tell you what happened? Are you kidding me? I was nearly killed. Then I was told that the maniac survived. He killed a great man that happened to be a very good friend before targeting me.

After everything happened I was stuck here and those asshole cops came and told me everything with no warning. He is still out there, the one thing I truly love to do almost killed me. Now I will never get to do again." She broke down again, blubbering for ten minutes before she was able to coherently get her thoughts out again.

"I know it is hard but there are many things you can still do even if dance is no longer a part of your life the way it used to be. Just because he came after you, because he is angry at the dance studio, doesn't mean he ruined your life. Kaylie you have to focus on the positive things in your life. You need to believe you are strong enough to get past all of this."

"Go to hell, you'll never understand." She turned away and closed her eyes. She fought the tears for as long as she could but gradually succumbed to the sorrow and frustration. She was never going to get it. Garrett was wonderfully supportive but she was sure he was never going to be able to completely understand either. She felt completely alone. It was horrible; she had no idea what she was going to do.

Cindy stood up, she wanted to push this but it was clear right now they weren't going to make any progress. She had had many patients over the years. Even now she had a couple that tugged at the heartstrings but watching Kaylie break down, hearing the continuous saga of what she was going through, was absolutely heart breaking. She fought off her own tears while she gathered her things. "We can talk later Kaylie, and you have your journal if you have anything you want to get out before tomorrow. Try to remember that those that love you only want the best and will be there for you no matter what."

When she was gone, and the crying was over, Kaylie fell asleep. She dreamt about the man that nearly killed her. The one that had, in her opinion, taken her life away. They were back in the cab, flying through the Chicago back roads at break neck speeds. The driver was already dead but somehow the cab drove on without him. "This is because of you," he told her, pointing at the slouched figure in the front seat. "If you hadn't stolen my show I wouldn't have to kill you and he would still be alive."

She tossed and turned, tears streaming down her contorted, unconscious face. The spasms became more violent as she tried to claw her way out of the nightmare. The words rang again in her ear; this is your fault. "It's my fault," she agreed. "It's my fault, I killed him and I should die for it."

She awoke with a start, screaming out in pain both physical and emotional. The door burst open as three nurses came flooding in. They looked at the distraught girl in the bed, trying to calm their own breathing. The oldest one stepped forward and tried to look comforting. "Did you have a bad dream, dear?"

Kaylie looked up through a haze of tears blurting out a single sentence. "I killed him."

The nurses exchanged wide-eyed glances then looked back at Kaylie. "What are you talking about, Miss Reynolds?"

There was no automatic correction now; Kaylie's entire body gave up. She fell back against the pillows stating again. "I killed him. It's all my fault. If not for me they would be alive. I killed him, I killed both of them."

The alarms were sounding loud and clear in the nurses' heads. The one closest to the door exited to place a call to Cindy. She left a voicemail then returned to the room. This was going to be a difficult day. The head nurse sedated Kaylie. When she had fallen asleep again, they restrained her arms. She then called for a security patrol to make sure when she woke back up she didn't try to hurt herself. She tried calling Cindy again but it still went straight to her voicemail.

Chapter 19

Meyar and Rommel came back to the hospital to try again to talk to Kaylie but were stopped by the medical staff. The head nurse that had medicated Kaylie asked them to step into the office. She explained the trance that she had fallen into following their previous visit. She mentioned the things she had been saying just before she was given the drugs to help her sleep. Their concern was evident but did not comfort her in anyway. She made it perfectly clear that they would not be allowed to speak with her until the psychologist felt she was prepared to handle it.

Meyar tried to impress upon her the importance of the information they sought but she was unmoved, no one would be talking to her today; that was final. Rommel gave her a card with both of their cell phone numbers printed on it. He asked that she keep them informed as to Kaylie's condition and when she may be available. She said she would but barely glanced at the card when she took it. Arms crossed over her chest she watched them leave.

She was so focused on the officers that she didn't notice the homeless man walking up the hall from the opposite direction. He walked slowly but deliberately. When he passed the detectives he turned his head away. She was satisfied that she had protected Kaylie from any further emotional strain today. The medication would be wearing off soon. She should be able to get Cindy in to talk to her and things could start to get better for the poor young dancer.

She sat down at the desk to work on scheduling assignments when the heart rate alarm went off in Kaylie's room. *Oh lord,* she thought, *she's having another nightmare.* Normally she would have let the patient sleep to get through it but after the terrible statements she had made after the last dream she thought it better to wake her. She crossed the hall and started to turn the handle on the door when she heard a man's voice coming through the door.

The nurse frowned. No one was supposed to be in there. She had stopped the officers, so who could it be? She flagged down one of the other nurses. Waving her over, they leaned in to hear more clearly. The voice was low and muffled through the thick oak door but it was definitely not coming from the television, someone was in the room.

"Go catch the detectives before they leave," she hissed urgently. "Tell them there is a man in Kaylie's room. We need their assistance. Hurry." She pushed the girl down the hall then turned back to the door debating on going in or waiting until the officers could do it. Something was going on in that room. She felt in her gut that it was wrong.

The man's voice continued but for a moment it was solo. Then when she pressed her ear directly against the door she could hear Kaylie. She wasn't talking; it sounded more like whimpering, as though she was crying or gagged. This was bad. She needed to do something but she didn't want to risk making the situation any worse.

"I am going to get you out of there safe," she whispered the promise. "If it's the last thing I do, I am going to make sure you're safe." She looked down the hall as she heard the heavy sound of running boots on the linoleum floor. She held up a hand for them to stop. Pressing a finger against her lips, she signaled to them to be quiet. She pointed at the door but the expression on her face told the entire story.

She temporarily breathed a sigh of relief that the officers were here but then realized Kaylie was in that room with someone and she was restrained. She couldn't defend herself. She stepped away from the door. She led the detectives into the small office across the hall again, filling them in on what she knew. Admittedly it wasn't much, but they agreed it was important that they make sure she was all right.

Meyar stepped up to the door and grasped the handle preparing to rush the room. He wanted take the man inside by surprise. He gently pressed down but there was no give, the door was locked. His eyes widened and without thinking he pressed again throwing his shoulder into the door. There was no surprise now. He hoped he got inside before anything happened to her.

Chapter 20

The man inside looked at the door then back at her, smiling his near toothless grin. "This is going to be fun," he told her.

He walked over and sat beside his sobbing hostage. She shuddered as he put a stinking arm around her shoulders. he held her trembling hand like they were friends. She hated him. This was the monster that nearly killed her, now he was here. Just the sight of him made her physically sick. His smell was so thick it filled the room. She felt like it was choking her. She wanted to scream but couldn't, partly because of the pillowcase he had shoved into her mouth and taped in, but mostly because of the gun he had sitting on the chair next to the bed.

The gun she didn't recognize. She expected the same one she had seen flash in the back of the cab but this one was smaller, black instead of silver. It looked just as deadly though. She was trying to keep herself under control but the panic was growing inside of her. He began rubbing her arm and she felt the bile rising in her throat. Swallowing hard she closed her eyes trying to tell herself that this was just another nightmare.

"How exciting for you to be here for the end?" His voice snapped her eyes back open. The end? He was back to finish what he had started in the cab. He was going to kill her. "She was supposed to give it to me, did you even know that?"

Kaylie had no idea what this lunatic was talking about but she didn't want to rock the boat, it was clearly already sinking. She couldn't help herself; she really wanted to ask what he was referring to. She felt her mouth attempting to ask without consent from her brain but was stopped by the gag. It didn't matter, he launched into the rant on his own.

"That bitch has always been jealous of me. I have been performing for years and will always be better than her. My stupid brother had to go and marry her and instead of investing in me he helps her open that joke of a company. Then I tell them I will agree to perform in the shows and what does she do? She makes me audition, bitch!" Screaming the word *bitch* resulted in jiggling sounds from the door and a knock coming through.

"Kaylie, can you hear me?" The man was muffled but his distinct voice came through loud and clear. She never thought she would have been happy to hear it. She didn't dare do anything to throw Nick off but she looked longingly at the door. He caught her gaze and smiled that terrible near toothless smile again.

"Don't worry; it will all be over soon. You know what she did when I went in to save that worthless place? She tells me that my vision doesn't match the theme of the show, that I am too extreme. What the hell is that?" He began pacing, she didn't want to be a part of this, but she was mesmerized. He stalked over to the chair snatching the gun from the seat. "Too extreme, can you believe that? I am an artist." He pounded his chest with his fist on every word for emphasis. "And then that moron musical director was so jealous of my abilities that he purposely played the acoustic version when I told him to use the recording I had handed him. He lied. He said there was nothing on the cd. It was his fault and then he got an attitude with me."

His pace picked up speed. He was waving the gun wildly now as his anger intensified. She kicked me out of the studio and I told her off. She deserved it but then my own brother kicked me out of his house, choosing that bitch of a wife over his own brother. He turned me out into the street because of her. She ruined everything."

She finally understood. When she joined the company she heard stories about the crazy guy that Sabrina had kicked out when he tried to take over the studio and recreate the company. She had never met him so had no idea until now as to what he looked like but the picture was becoming very clear. He hated Sabrina. He was determined to kill anything involved with her.

"I got arrested for stealing from a bakery, all I wanted was something to eat and they locked me up for three years because I had drugs on me and a gun. It wasn't even my gun but they took it when they locked me up. I tried to call my brother but he never returned the call or came to see me. But before he kicked me out I took that bitch's gun and kept it for a rainy day. They searched all of my stuff but they never found that gun." Holding up the gun in his hand he explained. "This one I stole from another guy on the street." He laughed.

She stared at him. He was terrible, so self-involved that he honestly believed all of this was an injustice toward him. He killed people. He was here to kill her all because he thought he was supposed to be in charge of Sabrina's company. He was getting lost in his own delusion and for a minute he seemed to have lost interest in her. She tugged on the restraints around her wrists but they were on tight. She thought there might be some give in the left one but not enough to slip her hand through.

Nick Marks kept pacing and mumbling to himself. Then after a few minutes he regarded her head on. "You know what? I think I may have finally gotten through to her when that bastard director died. It wasn't for fun, understand, it was just business. The business of justice. I am better than anyone in that place will ever be."

He walked straight to her and put his face right against hers. "You are being promoted as the new rising star and performing my show. That piece was mine but instead she gave it to a nobody like you. You are no rising star." He grabbed her chin hard in his grimy hand while he pressed his forehead even harder into hers'. "Look at you sitting here like the nobody you are."

He laughed a foul burst of breath in her face and her stomach turned. He straightened up casually strolling to the door while listening with delight to the rapid whispers coming from the other side. The phone in the room rang and he seemed to light up. This was getting complicated but it seemed to thrill him. The phone continued to ring but she barely heard it, her entire focus was on the madman in front of her.

"You know, I have known for a long time that the music I chose would create the best show opener. That's why I decided to show them how it's done. Then that bitch goes and throws it in my face by casting you and your shining worthlessness in my role. You are nothing and you are supposed to open my show? I don't think so."

He stalked back across the room. She watched as he began ranting to the wall as though it could hear him. The ringing stopped and she was able to pick up another sound, a chopping sound. She frowned, ignoring the raving man for a few moments until realized what it was, the propellers of a helicopter. It was hovering outside the window somewhere. Who could that be and what on earth did they want?

The phone began again. This time it made her jump. After several rings it dropped silent again. He said nothing just watched her. She was trying to keep the pillowcase from creeping down her throat; it was tripping her gag reflex but she was too terrified to move. When he turned back to his conversation with the wall she worked her arm against the restraint as quickly but quietly as possible. It was beginning to loosen and she thought if he was distracted long enough she might actually be able to get her left hand free.

He stopped talking but remained with his back to her. She began to sweat from nerves and the work she was doing. She almost had her hand free and was watching him closely. Just as she felt the strap give a little more he whipped around. She froze shaking in fear. He leapt across the room grabbing her by the shoulders. "It's happening; everyone is finally going to see me as the star I really am. That bitch is going to get exactly what she deserves."

He was grinning ear to ear and she saw the total disconnect from reality in his eyes. She began whimpering again in spite of herself. She didn't want to move or make a sound but there were people all around and the monster still had the gun in his hand. He took it and slid it on her arm. The icy metal chilling her to her core as the tears spilled over again. She had lived through the accident just to have him break in here and kill her anyway.

Chapter 21

Meyar was coordinating with the tactical team while Rommel was working to establish contact with Nick. The nurse had filled him in on the fact that she had been hysterical so they had restrained her. Now she was locked in the room with the man that tried to kill her and she couldn't fight back. There was a swarm of officers roving the hallway. After nearly half an hour of trying to get in contact they had gotten nowhere. He could only imagine how scared she was.

He looked down the hall and saw his concerns reflected in the face of Garrett. He and the rest of Chicago were aware of what was happening here. It had been front page, headline news when the accident happened. Then rehashed again when Justin Denton died; now here again were the makings of a tragedy involving the same cast of characters. He rubbed his eyes, doing everything possible to stay focused. He had made a promise; she was going to get out of there alive.

They received word that the blinds were drawn so there was no visual from the outside. He was not picking up the phone but every now and then they were able to hear screaming from inside. He seemed to be calling her names. That led Meyar to believe he was right on the edge but he didn't want to break down the door and risk him hurting her. The longer they waited the more of a chance he was going to do something drastic, but they had to be careful when and how they made their move.

"Detective, all efforts to establish a connection have failed and we cannot get a visual. What are we going to do?"

"I don't know Sargent," Meyar leaned his head against the wall. Taking a deep breath, he sighed. "I just don't know."

Chapter 22

Inside the room Nick was exuberant with glee at his chance to be the star of this nightmare. He pranced around the room and barley noticed her. She took a chance yanking hard with her left hand and heard something crack. Pain shot up her arm. Her hand was on fire but when she chanced a peek, she saw that she was free. He had his back to her so she reached up and pulled the pillowcase from her mouth. Just then he began to spin so she bit down then put her arm back hoping he wouldn't notice that it was no longer strapped.

He was oblivious. He kept dancing for another minute. Then he walked over to her and took her hand. "It's time." He told her and kissed her cheek. The touch of him made her skin crawl but she held her breath to keep from moving. He rushed to the door and pressed his ear against it, listening to see if anyone was directly on the other side of the door. He reached down, quietly unlocking the door. She heard the click and was completely thrown off.

Not only did he mean to kill her but also he intended to have an audience. She couldn't wait any longer; she reached over and undid the strap on her right hand then pulled the pillowcase from her mouth. She didn't scream though she desperately wanted to. She was going to fight as long as she could; she just had to wait for the right moment.

He walked back and stood next to the bed. He smiled and listened for the sounds of intruding officers. There was a scuffle of feet outside and he looked at her. "This is the end," he smiled. "I'm going to be a star, finally, the way I always should have been." He sighed, caught her eyes and raised the gun.

Chapter 23

Meyar asked Rommel to try one more time but it didn't look like anything was happening. The room had been quiet for a while now. That was making him very nervous. Garrett pushed his way through the gaggle of police. He was pacing near the desk a few feet away.

"What are we waiting for Detective?"

"Garrett, we don't want to risk startling him and having him do something rash. We have no visual confirmation of his whereabouts in the room. We cannot get him to pick up the phone. We're planning to enter the room but we want to do it the right way, do you understand?"

"Well do it already, my fiancé is in there and I can't live without her, do you understand that?" Garrett returned to his pacing. As he turned back toward the officers he was halted in his tracks.

The gunshot rang out, shattering the commotion of the hallway. After the split second of shock wore off Meyar jump across the hallway and threw himself against the door. Out of desperation he clutched the handle almost yelling out when it turned in his hand. Rommel had grabbed Garrett, muscling him back to keep him from rushing the room. Screams and shouts were echoing through the hallway as Meyar disappeared through the doorway and threw it closed behind him.

He saw the blood on the wall. He saw the gun on the floor but it took a second to realize that there was a sobbing, hyperventilating woman on the bed. He looked closely at the body on the floor; it was male. Nick Marks lay bleeding and dead on the floor of the hospital room. Kaylie, upon seeing the detective began to scream. Garrett fought free of Rommel when he heard Kaylie and rushed the room.

She was weak Crying and shaking, covered in blood, but she was alive. That was all he cared about. He hugged her tight and held her, not caring that her piercing screams were going to end up giving him a migraine. It was all worth it. He was just happy she was alive.

Just a few minutes behind him, Sabrina squeezed her way into the room. Officers had tried to hold her back but when she said who she was and gave the look that always snapped the dancers to attention, they wisely stepped aside allowing her access to the room. She waited patiently while Garrett hugged her then threw her own arms around Kaylie's neck, also ignoring the screams. She thought of the young dancer like a daughter. The fact that she survived gave her so much happiness she didn't know where to begin.

Detectives Meyar and Rommel finally cleared the room except for Garrett, who made it clear he was going nowhere. They sat down with Kaylie. When she was able to stop crying and yelling they tried to ask her some questions. The nurse had come in and, with Garrett and Sabrina's help, bathed Kaylie, getting all of the blood off her. She was quiet the entire time and just watched them work from recessed, haunted eyes.

She felt more like she was watching this all in a dream but the pool of blood still yet to be cleaned up on the floor was a ghostly reminder of the past few hours. He was gone. He was actually gone. He wasn't coming back to hurt her ever again. The gun had been bagged as evidence and his body bagged up then wheeled away. She felt the tugging as they pulled her clothes off and the heat of the water when they sponged away the gore but the sensations were only skin deep.

Now, fresh and clean, dressed in a new hospital gown, warm and dry she stared at the officers sitting across the room. They had asked to be alone with her but Garrett was clear, that was not going to happen. The nurses picked up on his tone as well. They told him that there were going to be no visiting hours tonight. He had left for twenty minutes to call her parents and fill them in on everything. He had been in contact off and on and they were watching television to try and get updates.

When the hospital called to inform him of the situation he decided to come without them. He knew it would be bad either way but he didn't want anyone else pacing the halls waiting for what could have been far more tragic. Her mother took the news with gratitude. Her father was angry for being kept away but thanked him for the update. When he was done he returned to Kaylie's side, waiting to talk to the detectives. Kaylie gave the slightest of smiles when he took his place next to her

Deep inside she was glad he was doing so well with everything. She would be happy once her emotions came back to the surface but right now they were more like memories of emotions that she would be able to access later. She blinked herself back to the present and shook her head, clearing the fog while trying to focus on the barrage of questions she knew would be coming at her.

Meyar surprised her. He walked over and hugged her before returning to his seat. She didn't hug him back, mostly because the action so completely caught her off guard she was in shock. She tried to smile but wasn't sure it came across; she was still numb. Once Garrett had come back, he sat on the bed with her and she put her head on his shoulder.

Garrett gently stroked her arm while she settled back into the bed. She closed her eyes breathing deep still shaking away the feel of his blood. She imagined that this nightmare had been exactly that. She wanted to believe she was home with Garrett on the couch drifting off during the evening news. It was a wonderful thought, but when she opened her eyes the officers were patiently watching her, bringing everything back with horrible detail.

"Kaylie?" Meyar started. "We need to talk to you about what happened today. Are you able to do that?"

"Do you really have to do this right now?" Garrett asked protectively.

"I'm very sorry but the sooner we get her statement the sooner we can let her rest and can wrap up the investigation. I think it would be best for everyone."

"It's ok baby." She patted Garrett's arm. "The sooner we get this started the sooner it will be over then we can get on with our lives."

"If you're sure you're up to it, honey; but if you start to feel like you want to stop then you just say so, okay?"

"Yeah baby, I will. Ok detective, so I'm guessing you want me to tell you everything that happened in here today." Kaylie told the detectives everything, from the sedation and restraints of the nursing staff to waking up gagged with Nick in her room. His rant about why he had gone after her and Justin to how excited he had been that he was going to be a star. He wandered around the room even talking to the walls.

She told them about pulling her arm free of the strap as well as risking pulling the gag out but he hadn't even noticed. She remembered the phone ringing and that he never seemed to even hear it. It hadn't seemed like he had come in to take her as a hostage but more to tell his story. He had been so happy when he heard everyone out in the hallway talking but then, just as quickly as the glee came on, his anger flashed about him being pushed aside.

He had made it very clear that Justin and Kaylie weren't the actual targets of his rage; he was merely using them as pawns to get his message across. All of his anger was directed toward Sabrina. He had called her a bitch several times, even screaming it once or twice. Meyar confirmed it had traveled through the door but they had thought he was yelling at her. She said no, he barely acknowledged her as a person. He seemed more to be in a trance, confessing why he had done what he had.

134

He mentioned a couple of times that the end was near and had paced back and forth waving the gun. She was sure he was going to kill her. He had mentioned getting out of town when he was in the cab but she now realized that he had just wanted to get away and not deal with life anymore. She thought that maybe he wanted to die in the crash and had been disappointed when he survived.

He came for her because she had also survived. He figured that by confessing his story to her beforehand, his story would be told and he would be the center of attention the way he always thought he deserved to be. He blamed Sabrina and Kyle for ruining his life. Just before he had put the gun to his head and pulled the trigger he had said that they killed him a long time ago; now his blood was on their hands.

The officers asked a couple more questions about the specifics but after a quick check to make sure she hadn't handled the gun herself they wrapped up their conversation closing their notebooks. Standing and shaking hands with both Kaylie and Garrett they prepared to leave. Just before he exited the room, though, Detective Meyar turned back to the couple.

"Congratulation on your upcoming wedding you two." He said with genuine emotion in his voice. "You're a great couple. I know after everything you have gone through, you can survive anything. You will be happy for a lifetime, I'm sure." He didn't wait for a response before leaving which was good, they were so stunned it took several minutes before either was able to voice a thought.

"I always thought he was kind of a jerk," Garrett murmured. "Now I'm not sure what to think."

"I know, he drove me crazy. He treated me like I was the one that caused the accident. He was sort of an ass and here he goes and says something sweet like that?" She laughed. "What a crazy day."

She laid back and closed her eyes, yawning. Now that it was over and she had a moment to relax, she realized how completely exhausted she was. Garrett could see that she was fading fast. He grabbed the bed controls, lowered the backrest of the bed and pulled the blanket up over them. "Are you staying with me tonight?" Kaylie whispered; her voice thick with sleep.

"Nothing could take me away. There is nowhere else I can imagine being. I want to make sure you have nothing to worry about." He slipped his arm under her neck and snuggled up beside her, burying his face in her hair. He didn't think he had ever loved her more than he did right then. He was more aware than he wanted to be as to just how close he came to losing her today.

If that madman had wanted to kill her instead of himself, there would have been nothing any of them could have done about it. He knew she was a fighter and a survivor but who knows what would have happened if it had come down to that. He breathed a ragged sigh and held her close allowing a few tears to escape and run across the bridge of his nose dropping onto the pillow. Her breathing had become deep and steady; she was even lightly snoring. He felt her heartbeat against his arm and felt his own syncing up as he drifted off to sleep.

Chapter 24

The next morning, with light streaming in through the now open blinds, Garrett awoke to a strange sight. There was Cindy beaming at him from the chair next to the bed. She wasn't talking just smiling and watching them sleep. There was a file open on her lap along with a cup of what smelled like lemon tea sitting on the table next to her with a thin wisp of steam wafting up from the rim.

"Creepy isn't it?" Kaylie asked from her position beside him. He jumped at the sound of her voice turning to look at her. She was stretching and rubbing her eyes.

"You knew she was here?" He was amazed, Kaylie hadn't looked past him and Cindy still hadn't said anything.

"She always does that. She comes in at some ridiculous hour then sits and waits for you to wake up. When you finally do she is sitting there with that stupid giant smile and it completely freaks you out, right?" He listened to the words but found it incredible that this was a habitual thing for them. He looked back at Cindy as he sat up and stretched. Cindy sat back, closed the file while sipping her tea.

"How are you feeling this morning Kaylie?" She asked looking past Garrett.

"I feel like I was strapped down and forced to listen to a maniac give me his life story before he splashed his blood and guts all over me."

"Well that's to be expected." Cindy said writing something down in the chart. "I talked to the doctors. They tell me that physically you are doing well now that you're eating again. Looks like you are going to be going home in a few days."

"Oh yeah?" Kaylie smiled at the news but them sobered. "And then what? What am I supposed to do once I get out of here? The injuries are still there and I still cannot dance so what am I supposed to do, huh?"

"I'm sure you will figure something out. You're very smart and you have a terrific support base, Kaylie. Your parents and Garrett will do everything they can for you, I imagine. Not to mention all of your friends."

"Yeah I guess." She was disheartened anyway. She had no idea how it was all going to be ok.

"Well I just came to check in on you and to let you know that you would be going home soon. This is going to be our last appointment while you're here but I would very much like to continue seeing you on a regular basis, say once a week? Does that sound good?"

"Yeah, sure, why not. We will find a time, not like I'm going to have a whole lot else to do."

"All right, wonderful!" Cindy exclaimed, clearly ignoring the sarcasm in Kaylie's tone. "We will have a lot of fun together I'm sure."

Kaylie said nothing, just rolled her eyes and held Garrett's hand. He had been silent throughout this entire exchange as if he was mesmerized by the situation. He put his arm around her shoulders and hugged her, kissing the top of her head. Cindy swept up her belongings then wandered out the door humming something to herself.

"That was the oddest thing I have ever seen, babe." Garrett said. He looked even more bewildered than he sounded. "You two do that everyday?"

"Something like that, yeah. She plays mind games, makes me mad, then when I snap. She tells me that we have made progress then she leaves. She left me some journals and had me write down questions I have or thoughts for us to go over but we never have. I'm pretty sure she never even looked at them. I just use them to vent about how lame the therapy is, how useless she is. Now she wants me to come see her once a week even after I get the hell out of here, lucky me."

"Well you've been through a lot. I'm sure you will be dealing with it for a long time so it's probably a good idea to talk to someone, but we can try to find someone else if you would be more comfortable with that."

"No, I have already been dealing with her so I know how she operates. If I have to talk to someone I may as well deal with the person I'm already familiar with, don't you think?"

"Sure, Kaylie, whatever you think is best. And she was right about one thing."

"Oh? What's that?"

"You do and will always have a strong support group, honey. Your family and friends love you very much. We are always going to be here to help you, no matter what you are doing."

"I know, it's just that it feels like I am in the middle of trying to figure out how to completely reinvent myself and nothing else I have ever done has felt so completely me as dancing has."

"I understand, baby. I still think it may be possible for you to recover enough to find something dance related to do."

"Yeah, maybe." She smiled but he could see she was far away now, lost in thought.

"I need to get going Kaylie," He stood up and heard his joints cracking. He bent and kissed her lips deeply and passionately. Pressing his forehead to hers he looked into her eyes. "I love you."

"I love you too." She smiled but she knew he was being as serious as he could. "Thank you Garrett, for everything you do for me."

He kissed her again then headed out before he started to cry. It was dumb but he hated to cry in front of her. He just wanted to be strong, that was what she needed right now. She watched him go and considered going back to sleep when she was interrupted. A doctor came into the room and sat down beside her.

"Are you ready for your evaluation?" He asked her.

"My evaluation?" She has totally confused.

"Physical therapy, we are going to evaluate you to see where you are physically so we know how to plot out your course of treatment."

"Really, that's today? Don't you know what happened yesterday?"

"Yes I saw the news just like the rest of the greater Chicago area."

"So how can you think I would be ready for something like this today?"

"Well you weren't physically injured during the confrontation and you have been healing for several days. The sooner we get going on this the sooner you will be able to get out of here." There was no moving this man. She wanted to keep pressing the issue but a nurse showed up with a wheelchair to take her down to the rehabilitation room.

Seeing that arguing was getting her nowhere she did everything she could but every activity hurt and she was terribly weak. Even something as simple as standing was almost unbearable with the fractures to her legs. She had braces on. She was supposed to be able to walk with them while the healing finished but she had to lean so much on the support bars it felt more like she was dragging her legs, not walking. She cried but the doctor just kept telling her more things to try. It was humiliating. It was painful. As far as she could remember it was the worst hour of her entire life outside of the cab. Her wrist was on fire from wrestling it free from the restraints; by the end she was soaked in sweat and barley hiding her tears.

When she was finally permitted to return to her room, she had been given a cane and a small booklet to read over that would explain what they thought of her current condition. She also had another book that listed her exercises as well as how long it was

140

going to take to get past each step of the recovery. She skimmed them, not really taking in the information until she came across one sentence in the overall evaluation, "Will most likely have permanent limitations in flexibility and strength in back and legs resulting from stress suffered during crash."

So that was it, it was permanent. All of the pain she felt from exerting herself would always be there in some form. Why even bother with the exercises if she wasn't going to get better? Most of these things were exercises she had been doing for years. Now it was almost impossible to even complete one of them let alone the entire workout. She felt herself slipping into a deep funk but it was too late, she couldn't stop it. For what felt like the millionth time she covered her face with her hands and cried.

She was alone in the room for more than an hour but that didn't matter, she was still crying when the nurse came in to check on her. She mistakenly took the tears as a sign of her remembering the tragic scene from the day before and shook her head. When she left the room she called Cindy to let her know the situation.

Cindy listened politely but felt that the analysis was wrong and that since she had been undergoing physical therapy for the first time today it was more likely the shot of reality that was affecting her. She told the nurse that she was going to make a call and have someone come and visit Kaylie. That it should help. She agreed, though was doubtful. She hung up. An hour or so later, the visitor arrived and headed into Kaylie's room. The nurse made a mental note to go check on her in a couple hours to see if it had actually helped.

"Sabrina, what are you doing here," Kaylie sniffled.

"I got a call that you were crying again. Your therapist thought I would be able to help."

"I don't want to cry in front of you."

"Then don't. But as long as I'm here you could at least tell me why you were crying in the first place."

"You wouldn't understand." Kaylie laid back. She turned her face away hiding the fresh batch of tears threatening to fall. How could she tell the woman that was her idol that she couldn't make it through a workout she had done a million times. Sabrina was physically the strongest person Kaylie had ever known; this would just let her down. "I don't understand why you even bother with me. I am not part of the dance company anymore."

"Oh? Are you quitting? I would have thought you would have told me before now. I guess I should just leave you alone then, although I am curious as to why you want to leave us."

"What? I didn't quit. I was in the accident. The doctors said I was done, my injuries were probably going to be permanent."

"Oh, I didn't realize that you were probably permanently injured, how could I ever understand that?" Sarcasm dripped from every word as she rolled her eyes. She kicked her feet up on the edge of the bed and watched with interest as Kaylie tried to figure out how to respond.

"I just went through physical therapy earlier and barely made it. I can't even walk without leaning on the bars so they gave me a stupid cane. A cane! I used to be a dancer."

"See there you go again, used to be. Can you just tell me out loud that you are giving up and a quitter so I can stop worrying and trying to help you? That way I can go put effort into those that still care about themselves and their lives."

"I don't want to tell you that," Kaylie whined. "I'm not a quitter, I do care it isn't my fault."

"Kaylie, you are not the only dancer that has ever been injured or been told that something may or may not get better." Sabrina snapped at her. "We make our own choices. We make our own destinies. If you are prepared to give up on yourself then I am wasting my time here and I wasted the last year on you. I know you have what it takes to overcome this, to dance again. But what I think means nothing unless you believe it too."

"How can you be so sure that I could get better?" Kaylie was amazed by the outburst but felt compelled to see what else she had to say. Instead of answering right away Sabrina took off her sweater and turned around facing away from Kaylie. She lifted the back of shirt and there along the right side of her spine was a crude, jagged scar close to five inches long. Kaylie's eyes opened even wider as Sabrina took the shirt completely off and she saw that there were two more long scars on either side of the spine between her shoulder blades.

"Oh my god, Sabrina, what happened? How did you get those scars? And how is it possible that I didn't know you had them?"

"I was in an accident too. And I imagine that you have never noticed that I either wear sweaters over the leotards or ones with closed backs at rehearsals." She had to admit that Sabrina's dance attire had never been something she paid a lot of attention to; mostly she had just loved to watch her move. Kaylie aspired to one day be able to perform on the same level.

"What happened in your accident?"

"I was young, only seventeen and had been at a party with friends. None of us had been driving very long and it was late. We had all been drinking because my best friend had snuck some vodka from her mom's liquor cabinet. We mixed it with our sodas and fruit juices. We had a good time but we had no idea just how drunk we were. When we left to go back to my house for the sleep over I was having I could barely walk to the car." Sabrina's eyes were distant, as she talked they began to mist. She was obviously trying not to cry but it wasn't working. Kaylie wondered why she would cry, she clearly made it through the accident ok, but she didn't dare interrupt the story so she waited quietly for Sabrina to continue.

"There were three of us, Nicole, she was my best friend; Rose was her little sister, she was two years younger than us and did everything Nicole did. And of course I was there. Nicki and I were

143

barely conscious after all we had to drink but Rose only had a couple and seemed ok to us. She got behind the wheel and Nicki sat with her up front but kept turning around to talk to me. The radio was up. We laughed and sang along, only having to go a few miles to get to my house; we weren't paying much attention. There was hardly anyone out that late anyway. Driving down my road it seemed really dark, no street lights on country roads you know; anyway, Rose yelled something but with the music I didn't hear her so I sat up to ask her what she said. She turned around to tell me and right then a couple big deer jumped out of the trees and into the road.

I screamed for her to turn around. She honked the horn and jerked the wheel. The deer jumped away. We never hit them but as she tried to swerve back and get stable on the road she overcompensated. We went into the ditch on the opposite side of the road. She put the front in so hard and fast that the car flipped over. I was able to undo my seatbelt and crawl up to the road but Nicole and Rose were trapped in the car. I yelled for help. After a minute or two a man came down the road. He called the police and ambulance but Rose died before they got to her." The tears were flowing now, she gave up attempting to stop them.

"What happened to your friend?" She wasn't sure she should ask but she had to know everything, Sabrina had been through so much but never let it show.

"Nicole?" Her voice was coming from a long way away.

"Yes, you said her sister died, but what happened to her? Did the paramedics get to her in time or did she die too?"

"Oh yeah, the paramedics got there. They got her out of the car. She was screaming about Rose. They had to sedate her on the way to the hospital." Sabrina was still distant but her voice had a hard, bitter edge to it. "I tried to jump in the ambulance with her but the guys working on me said I couldn't go. They put me in a different ambulance and drove away. Our parents were called and met us

144

there. I was treated, then after surgery to remove glass and put pins in parts of my back where it had fractured from being thrown, I was released. I tried to go see Nicole but when I walked into her room she screamed at me to get out. Said that she never wanted to see me ever again."

"Why would she say something like that? You guys were best friends."

"She blamed me. It was my car and I gave Rose the keys. I was also the one that had been talking to her when the deer jumped out in front of us. When she was released and went back home she went into Rose's room and took her entire bottle of pain killers." Sabrina turned to face the horrified young dancer. "She died in Rose's bed. She couldn't take the fact that her sister died and she never talked to me again."

"Oh my god Sabrina, you have been through so much. I can't imagine going through all of that and still doing everything you have."

"The picture you look at when you walk in the studio, the one of the two little girls in their leotards at the barre; that is me and Nicole in our first dance class." Kaylie's eyes closed as she tried to bring the image of the picture to her mind. She could see them, two smiling four year olds in black leotards and pink tights with pink ballet slippers on. They had to reach above their heads just to put their hands on the barre but they were trying and smiling at the camera as they did their best ballet pose. Kaylie loved that picture, she had always thought of herself as the little blond one but now she knew that the little blond girl had come to a tragic end so felt a part of herself lost.

"That is terrible, but you kept dancing."

"I dance for Nicole. She couldn't handle what happened and never forgave me but I dance to show her that the thing we loved is still alive. She will always live in me. She makes me the performer I am and always have been. You remind me of her you know, the way you look and the beautiful way you dance. But I see myself in you too, Kaylie. The doctors told me I was never going to dance again. My back was wrecked. After surgery it hurt to even sit or stand for long periods of time but I never let it stop me. I have always known who I am and what I was meant to do. Now let me see that in you; show me I was right. I know you're a fighter. You can beat this if you really want to. Please don't become like Nicole and give up."

Kaylie was crying. Sabrina had seen in her exactly what she had always aspired to be. She had wanted to be just like this amazing woman. Sabrina felt like she was exactly that. She cried for the tragic end of a young life and the horrible loss of a sister and a friend. She cried because she wanted so desperately to make Sabrina happy, to make her prediction true. She wanted to overcome the injuries and to one day dance again.

"I promise I will make you proud Sabrina. I am not a quitter." Sabrina was crying too.

"Good, then I will be there to help every step of the way. When you're ready you will have a home at the Marks Dance Company waiting to welcome you back. I will let everyone know you are doing better." She leaned down and hugged Kaylie tight sniffing back another sob. Pulling back she cupped Kaylie's face in her hands. "You listen to me, you have love and support from your family and friends, but most importantly you have strength inside you. You are the one that will beat this. You can overcome all the obstacles that have been put in front of you. It is going to be hard as hell girl, don't for a second think it won't, but you can do it."

"I will do it. It is going to be hard and hurt a lot but I am going to do it." The more she said it the more resolve she felt behind the words. "I am going to dance again. I am going to come back and be the best dancer you have ever seen."

Kaylie smiled. Sabrina smiled back. Wiping away tears she walked to the door and grabbed her coat off the hook. "I don't show many people my scars but I'm glad you know. If there really is some of me in there I better keep my eye on you, you might just own the studio someday."

That took Kaylie by complete surprise. Her smile grew even wider. "I'm coming for it Sabrina, you can count on it." When Sabrina left, Kaylie leaned back and thought over everything they had talked about. She hurt all over from the stretches and training she had attempted but right now she barely noticed it. She was focused on Sabrina's story. Kaylie was inspired by what a survivor her mentor was. Right then and there Kaylie made herself a promise; she would keep her word to Sabrina, she wouldn't give up. She would fight her way back to the studio.

Chapter 25

Kaylie was released to go home a few days later. While she wasn't looking forward to it, she vowed to go to all of her appointments with Cindy and do all of her physical therapy, no matter how much it hurt. Garrett had done exactly as he said, he set up an area in the living room with all of the resistance bands and balance balls along with a yoga mat and some light free weights; he really had gone all out. She was touched but not surprised; he was always going over the top for her. She called her mom and talked for hours even catching up for nearly an hour with her dad.

Once she was settled in they had dinner, she sat at the table, making a salad while he prepared steak and potatoes, one of their favorites. Neither one liked salad very much but she was determined to be helpful somehow. She thanked him for the workout area and he kissed the top of her head. After a relatively quiet dinner he went into the bedroom to grab the binder she had been keeping for wedding planning. He put it down in front of her and she smiled, flipping through it. They had been making so much progress on their planning before the accident, now she was going to have to work to get caught back up.

Over the next couple days she made calls, set up times to do cake tastings, made sure the invitations were going to be in on time, confirmed the time to figure out the menu for the reception as well as a time for a walk through. She was still using the cane and could only limp along for small periods of time. She was limited to short distances but she was looking forward to getting to make all of the last adjustments and designing the layout.

Her wedding was one of the biggest things keeping her going; she knew exactly what she wanted to make happen. She was planning to surprise Garrett at the reception and she called Sabrina to come over for coffee and ask for her help. A few days later she and Garrett went out to take care of all the appointments she set. She happily checked things off the list and added menus and sample invitations to her binder. She was able to walk through the hall with only a couple painkillers to make it through the entire day.

Things were coming together. She also found she was feeling more like her old self. Days went by and as the days turned into weeks she found herself getting more and more excited about the wedding. She got up every morning, pushing herself on the exercises. She did lighten up some on the weekends but still did her best to make sure she was improving each and every time.

The weekly therapy appointments she had come to look forward to as well. At first it was still just banter between the two women. As much as she found it intriguing to see if she could get under Cindy's skin she also noticed that, anytime she took the advice of her therapist, things did go a little easier for her. Her realizations did not necessarily come as a breakthrough but instead as small epiphanies that made her loosen up and become more cooperative over time. She also kept her journal going. She wrote her story and kept adding to it from the day she got the solo to the path through recovery.

She wanted to share them but wasn't sure how or with who, so she kept them to herself for months. But as the wedding date approached she traveled home for her final fitting and spent time with her family. While she was there she had an idea. She called a friend that now worked in publishing, asking her to lunch at the café down the street. After an hour or so of catching up, and a quick congratulations on the wedding, she got down to business. She presented her old friend with a few pages from one of her journals and explained her idea to make a book about what she had gone through and the fact that she recovered.

Her friend was very interested. She explained that she also had talked to Sabrina and convinced her to also get her story out there.

After reading the offered pages her friend looked at her for a long time. Finally she placed them aside before getting up to give Kaylie a huge hug. Her words, she told her, made her want to cry for what she had been forced to endure. The fact that she was capable of creating such a moving and graphic visual with the way she wrote made this a book that she couldn't wait to read. She said that if Sabrina wrote her story as well, or if Kaylie wanted to help her write her story as well she would be very interested in pitching both ideas to her boss.

Kaylie was so excited she called Sabrina from the restaurant to give her the good news. Sabrina was hesitant to write her story but when Kaylie told her that the publisher would still be interested if she wrote it on her behalf she brightened and agreed instantly. Kaylie thanked her friend and told her she would type up the book draft then send it to her as soon as possible. She said she would send Sabrina's soon as well, though that one may be following the wedding. They hugged one more time before she called her mother for a ride back home.

Finishing up the weeklong visit she kissed her mom and dad goodbye then slept the entire train ride back. She awoke with a start to the ringing of her phone, looking at the caller ID. It was Garrett, which meant she must be about 20 minutes from the station. It was what they had always done; they called fifteen to twenty minutes out to make sure the other was awake and had enough time to gather everything before their stop came up. She smiled, put the book she had been planning to read away and zipped up her bag.

When the train pulled in to the station she put the shoulder strap over her head and let it hang across her chest. She snatched the handle of her rolling suitcase with one hand using the other to handle her cane. She shuffled off the train, lunging into Garrett's welcoming arms. He wrapped her in a bear hug and took the suitcase for her; helping get everything to the cab he had waiting for them. She walked up and waited while he gave the driver the suitcase to put in the trunk, while she waited she repeated to herself that Nick Marks was gone and couldn't hurt her. She knew it would be years, if ever, before she got past her fear of taxis but she was doing her best to face those fears head on.

Home they went where she continued working on her physical therapy every day. The wedding was just around the corner and she was determined to make sure Garrett's surprise was ready. She skipped her last psychology appointment instead putting in extra time in her home gym but she did call Cindy to make sure she was going to come to the wedding. The guest list had definitely changed since the accident. It meant a lot to Kaylie that Cindy was going to be a part of it.

She went over the guest list and checked off who had and hadn't RSVP'd to come to either the ceremony or the reception then took the final headcount to the caterer at the hall. She confirmed with the minister before making sure her two bridesmaids had their dresses and the fittings had gone well.

One week before the wedding she went to pick up her mom and dad from the train station. They got to the hotel and got settled in while Kaylie tried on her dress. It took her awhile to get in the dress. Once she was done she turned to the three pairs of shoes she brought. The original pair was three inch white heels. They were beautiful and matched the dress perfectly but she was sure that it would be far too difficult to walk in them especially with her cane.

Her mom helped her but they both agreed that the three-inch pair would put too much strain on her. Next she jumped down to half-inch heels, but they made walking difficult because the dress dragged on the floor. She finally got the two-inch heels on and though they took much longer to get on, they seemed to fit better. She felt much more stable in them. They were low enough she didn't have to hunch with the cane but it kept the dress floating just above the ground when she walked.

The following day her mother and bridesmaids came over along with Sabrina and a few of the female dancers from the studio for a small, intimate bridal shower. There was joking and chatting with coffee and snacks everyone brought. Even though everyone had been told not to bring anything, each showed up with a gift. They brought her earrings and a necklace, the ones she had wanted for the wedding. She got a gift certificate for a massage and day of beauty. She was thrilled everyone's generosity would make it possible for her to be able to get her nails, hair and makeup done for her wedding day and then have the massage when her back and legs were stronger. She got a beautiful candle set and a journal with slots for pictures to use on their honeymoon. They were going to take a cruise to the Caribbean for a week. She was looking forward to going snorkeling and spending time in the water.

Sabrina gave her a camera that was waterproof so she could use it during the snorkeling. She was so excited that she nearly jumped off the sofa to hug her. Then it was her mom's turn, she handed Kaylie a check, it was enough for their wedding and honeymoon as well as paying bills for the past couple months. She knew they had been tight and was determined to help them out. This unexpected generosity brought tears to her eyes. Sabrina smiled, telling her that there was one more surprise for her but she wouldn't get it until she got back from her honeymoon and developed the film from the disposable camera they were using for the shower.

It seemed an odd thing to give as a gift, a picture, but she had come to fully trust both her parents and Sabrina so she pushed the curiosity out of her mind for the time being. They wrapped up the shower with a toast and everyone telling her how great she seemed to be recovering as they headed for home. Her mom left to go meet her dad for dinner while Sabrina moved to the chair near her workout area.

Kaylie went back to her exercises while they talked. Sabrina commented several times about her flexibility returning and how her strength seemed to be growing as well. They talked about her progress for another half hour or so then she turned on the recorder she had gotten so they could talk about everything Sabrina shared and the details of how she had continued on to become the woman that she was today. It still brought tears to her eyes every time she heard the story but she knew how inspiring it would be for others going through rough times. It had certainly helped her.

Chapter 26

The day of the wedding she woke up at five in the morning with an excitement she could feel all over. She was shaking as she got up checking and double-checking to make sure she had everything ready to go. At seven her mom came to pick her up so her day of beauty could begin. She was pampered like a princess getting a manicure and pedicure. Once her nails were ready she got her hair done and even though she knew she could do her own makeup it was nice to get the facial that came along with the makeup application.

By three o'clock she was primped and pampered, ready to go to the hall. They were having the ceremony and reception in the same hall with a couple hours in between for pictures at Millennium Park as well as along the water. While they were having the pictures taken the staff would be converting everything over. The ceremony was set up and she was dressed, she couldn't wait to get everything started.

"Are you ready honey?" Kaylie's mom took her hand. She squeezed it, looking at her daughter with concern.

"More than I have ever been for anything." She patted her mom's hand. She looked up as one of the ushers came into the bridal suite. "I think it's time for you to go sit down mom."

She left with the usher and Kaylie could hear the music starting. As her mom disappeared through the doors, the song changed and she could hear 98 degrees drifting down the hallway to her. It was the song that her bridesmaids were walking to; it was starting. Her dad stepped up beside her and put his hand on her shoulder, a way of comforting her he had always done. She loved knowing he was there.

"I have a surprise for you Akaylia." She turned around at the sound of her full first name. He stepped aside, there standing behind him, was her younger brother. He had never responded to her about whether he would be able to make it from Florida to come to the wedding. He was dressed in a tux and his girlfriend was with him dressed like the bridesmaids.

"Oh my god, Christian, you made it!" She practically squealed. She then looked at Michelle. "Michelle, why are you two dressed like that?"

"We talked to Garrett. He said it would be fun to add one more couple to the wedding party." Michelle told her. She was clinging to his arm carefully holding him and it was an awkward pose; Kaylie was so excited to see her little brother that it almost slipped by.

"Michelle, what is going on with you? You're standing strange, something is off about you."

"Actually we are happy to get to walk with you in your wedding because it will be good practice for ours," Christian answered for her. Kaylie's eyes widened with joy as Michelle moved her hands to reveal the gorgeous diamond ring that now adorned her left hand. She leaned heavy on her cane and hugged the bride-to-be. It was incredible to be able to see them so happy.

"This is so wonderful. Congratulations you guys!"

"Hey sis, I'm looking forward to talking to you more about this, all you want, but right now I think we are supposed to be walking down the aisle and waiting for you." He smiled and hugged her. "You look beautiful."

He kissed her cheek and took Michelle's arm leading her toward the music. Once they had turned the corner she heard the thrilled gasps at the sight of her brother in his fitted tuxedo. Then her father took her arm. He slowly walked with her, while she clutched her cane, and they made their way to the aisle. The bridal march started and she stepped to the head of the aisle.

They moved with the music and the cane never became the crutch it so rightfully could have. Her dad did cry a little during the

155

handoff but he stood proudly next to her mother after giving her away. Using Garrett as her stabilizer Sabrina came up and pulled her cane down to the front row so it wouldn't be in the pictures. The preacher welcomed everyone then gave the opening speech about what marriage means.

After a few readings and a poem written and read by Kaylie's mother, he asked for the rings and the vows. Garrett and Kaylie wrote their own vows. They wanted to give the same vow so wrote them together, each taking a turn reciting them. Once the vows were done, they exchanged the rings then Garrett leaned over and kissed her.

The minister laughed, "I guess he couldn't wait to kiss his bride."

"Look at her, how could anyone resist?" Garrett kissed her again as everyone laughed and clapped.

"Well since we skipped ahead to the kiss, I guess it only makes sense that by the power vested in me by God and the state of Illinois; I now pronounce you husband and wife. Go ahead and kiss her again, just to make it official." He smiled as Garrett kissed her deep, holding her close. Once again everyone laughed and clapped. "And now it gives me great pleasure for me to introduce for the very first time ever Mr. and Mrs. Garrett and Akaylia Michaels."

The music picked up again as they walked arm in arm down the aisle with Sabrina discreetly handing off the cane to help her. She smiled at her, so incredibly proud. They got to the limo and piled in, the bridesmaids and groomsmen, now including her brother and future sister in-law, her parents and his and of course the newlyweds. It was a warm, glorious day in early June. She was enjoying everything so much. Everyone always told her to be ready for things to go wrong at her wedding but so far nothing had been a problem; it was just getting better and better.

Pictures went quickly and after only forty-five minutes they were on their way back to the hall. When they arrived the DJ announced each pair that had walked down the aisle ending with Garrett and

Kaylie. They immediately moved into the toasts before dinner was even served because Kaylie requested the change. The maid of honor said a few nice words and the best man wished them a long and happy life. Garrett thanked everyone for all of the love and support they had received, then as he was about to hand the microphone back to the DJ, Kaylie wobbled to her feet and held out her hand for her microphone.

Garrett hesitantly handed it over before sitting down. She put her hand on the back of her chair as a support base, looking at her guests, smiling. "I just wanted to take a minute to say thank you for everything you have all done for us. Everyone here knows that earlier this year I was involved in an accident and with what was on the news most know the outcome. What you may not know is that I was told my injuries were going to be permanent and that I may not ever recover, even emotionally."

She lowered her head for a moment collecting her strength. "I found the faith and comfort from my friends so wonderful and have been working very hard to get better. One thing I had that helped me was inspiration through my wonderful friend and mentor Sabrina Marks, Sabrina can you stand up please?" Sabrina humbly stood up and nodded to Kaylie. "When I went through my first physical therapy appointment it hurts so badly I could barely move. I was ready to give up. She then took the time to tell me a story about a tragedy she had been involved in when she was a teenager and how she overcame it to become the amazing woman she is today."

All eyes turned to Sabrina, most expected her to take her seat again but she remained standing. Kaylie let go of the chair and grabbed her cane, walking to the center of the dance floor in front of the head table. She stood in the middle where Sabrina came up and hugged her. "I met with a friend of mine that works in publishing a few months ago and she has agreed to publish the incredible story that inspired me as well as the story of what I went through. I would say that what I have done is not as special but I can hope that between the two of us we can help to show others that it is possible to get past anything if you just believe, work hard, and have faith in those supporting you."

She looked back at the DJ and smiled nodding. "Garrett can you come and join me for a minute? I am feeling a big need to have our first dance now." He waited for a moment but when he heard the music start he walked around the table. He looked concerned. He stood at the edge of the floor, leaning toward her.

"Are you sure you want to try this? I don't want you to get hurt." His brow furrowed, as he looked her up and down. She stepped back and giggled.

Into the microphone she said, "I am sure I want to do this, as a matter of fact I have a surprise for you. I've been working with Sabrina everyday doing my physical therapy and I know I'm ready for this." He walked forward and held her making sure not to hit her cane. "You know what, there is one thing that I do need to do though." She turned back to Sabrina who was still standing on the edge of the dance floor. She smiled and Sabrina smiled back, knowingly.

"What is it you need Kaylie?"

"I need to get rid of this cane; it's just going to get in my way." She tossed the cane to Sabrina, who took it and finally went to sit down. Everyone's jaws dropped as she spun around and held Garrett. "It's ok baby, don't worry. I know exactly what I'm doing."

He still hesitated and the DJ started the song over. She began to move and after a moment of amazement he came forward and held her as they performed their first dance exactly the way it had originally been choreographed. Everyone stood and cheered as the song ended and he lightly dipped her with a kiss. He hugged her tight, tears in his eyes. He was so impressed and in awe of her recovery. He felt so happy to be able to spend the rest of his life with her.

With her surprise out of the way, dinner was served. All of the guests ate and drank to their heart's content. There was dancing and the cutting of the cake, all of the normal parts of a wedding, but then the DJ announced there was someone with a surprise for the bride. All eyes turned back to the dance floor to see Sabrina standing there with the microphone in her hands. She was smiling as a single tear escaped her eyes and rolled down her cheek.

"Kaylie can you come up here please?" Kaylie made her way through the crowd to the dance floor and looked at her idol with wide, unblinking eyes. "Akaylia Reynolds joined my dance company not that long ago and has easily become a budding young star. She is incredible to watch and an inspiration to be around. She is genuine and loves dance almost as much as that handsome new husband of hers." Everyone clapped and though she was telling everyone her news, Sabrina never took her eyes off Kaylie.

"Six months ago a monster tried to hurt me by destroying the lives of the people I love. He killed our musical director and we all miss him very much. He also tried to take this amazing light from the world and dash its brilliance. But he failed because she is a survivor. The day that she was hijacked this poster was put up around the city announcing the summer show for our studio." Sabrina unrolled the promotional poster, showing the crowd. "Kaylie, can you read what it says across the top for me please?"

"It says 'With opening performance solo by Akaylia Michaels.'" She looked at Sabrina with tears stinging the corners of her eyes. This was going to be the thing that ruined her wedding day; she had to be reminded of how far she still had to go.

"That's right, and yesterday while you were doing your last minute preparations and Garrett was helping you and your parents, this poster went up to replace it. Please read the top part again." Kaylie didn't want to read it, this was too much and she didn't want to hurt during the happiest day of her life. But she figured Sabrina had a good reason for doing this so she would go along for now.

"This one says," she leaned in with her eyes widening. "This one says that 'the opening number will be performed by Chicago's sweetheart survivor Akaylia Michaels'. How can that be?"

"The picture I wanted you to develop when you got home is of this poster. Kaylie I never recast the show, when you started to recover and I saw the determination you had I knew you would dance with us again. If you are feeling up to it then we will have you with us on opening night in six weeks. We just pushed it back and made it a summer concert series instead of an early summer recital. I had faith in you all along and decided I couldn't wait for you to know."

Kaylie couldn't believe it. She was going to be back on stage in just six weeks! Sabrina went on to tell everyone that all of her friends and family would receive a guest pass through will call and she would get each and every one of their names so that they could see her dance. She did mention that some of the more difficult numbers had been redone because she knew that there hadn't been enough recovery time yet but it wouldn't be long, she was sure of that.

Epilogue

The night ended perfectly and as her guests continued to party the night away, she and her new husband took the limo to the airport where they left on their honeymoon. The cruise was spectacular and she filled up the memory card that came with her new camera with pictures of tropical fish and Caribbean sunsets. They took part in every activity the boat had to offer, deciding that they would definitely be making cruises a regular part of their vacation experiences. Kaylie bought her family souvenirs while Garrett took pictures to turn into a scrapbook for his parents.

When they got home they all had brunch before Christian and Michelle had to head back to school. They had all talked about their upcoming nuptials and loved their gifts. Kaylie and Garrett went home to open the rest of their wedding presents then Kaylie immediately got to work on the thank you notes. Garrett laughed as he handed her the address book. "Why are you writing them now? We have plenty of time."

"No baby, I don't. I go back to rehearsal the day after tomorrow." She beamed at him but the smile faded when she saw his look of concern. "Honey, I told you, I'm ready for this."

"I just want to make sure you aren't trying to take on too much, too fast, that's all."

"I know you're concerned but I know my body and I'm ready. It'll be difficult at first and I promise I will not push myself further than I can actually take. I will be good but this is who I am and I know I'm ready." He leaned down and kissed her knowing he stood no chance of convincing her otherwise. She was determined to do this. He knew better than to stand in her way.

She finished the thank you cards and mailed them out by the following evening joking it was probably a thank you note record. She opened the closet that night, pulling out her dance bag for the

161

first time in months. Slowly unzipping the top she examined the contents of the bag. She had her tights, leotard, warm up pants and tank top, sports bra and all of her shoes. She also had her mp3 player that was no doubt sitting with a dead battery.

She fished it out and saw she was right so she plugged it in then went back to the bag making sure she had her braces and painkillers as well as three bottles of water ready. She set the alarm before going to bed that night but still woke up every hour or so to check that it was set correctly. She gave up on sleep around four thirty, getting up to start stretching. She made breakfast for herself and some for Garrett around seven. After they ate he jumped in the shower. She kissed him goodbye and left for rehearsal.

She didn't expect anything big, but the entire studio turned out for her return and she hugged each and every person that was a part of the world she loved. Rehearsal was brutal. She knew it would be a struggle but she reminded herself that at one point it was nearly impossible to walk. She kept at it and by the six-week mark she felt like she was ready for opening night.

That night she stood with Sabrina in the wings and looked out at the darkening auditorium. "I'm nervous Sabrina." She murmured as she saw familiar faces filing into their seats.

"I know you are, but you've come so far. I've been watching you in the studio. I wouldn't let you go on if I thought for even a moment you weren't ready."

"I know and I trust you. It's just that I don't want to let those people out there down."

"Once the music starts and they see you move there will be no way possible for them to be let down. You're an inspiration to each and every person sitting in that audience and you are an inspiration to me Akaylia Michaels."

"You really mean that?"

"I saw Nicole in you from the moment we met but I knew that even though she gave up, there was enough of me in you to keep

162

that from happening. She was an amazing dancer and I see her move every time I watch you. You have brought my best friend back to life for me and for that I can never repay you."

"Well you gave me the strength to get back up and dance again so I'm going to say we are pretty much even," Kaylie looked at her. "I made you a promise and you made me one back, tonight we are making both come true."

"You're exactly right," Sabrina hugged Kaylie the way her mom did when she got emotional. "Now I want you to go out there and dance your heart out. This is all for you. Forget the audience and forget about me. Dance for that husband of yours sitting there proudly in the front row. Dance for the girl that was told she would never walk without a cane and dance as the girl that stood up and said I'm a survivor and proved it."

Kaylie was stunned by the way Sabrina had of motivating the dancers with her pep talks. She closed her eyes and took a deep breath letting it out slowly while Sabrina walked out into the spotlight at center stage. She gave a brief background about the pieces to be performed that night then named the performers that the audience would be going on the journey with. She thanked them for coming and supporting the dancers. She welcomed them to opening night, giving a special welcome to the family and friends of the performers. Everyone clapped as she headed backstage again.

The light dimmed and the audience applause died down. Kaylie and Sabrina embraced once more for luck then Kaylie smiled as she walked onto the dark, bare stage. It was a simple but quick piece. She had practiced it multiple times in the previous weeks but this was the real thing. Her heart raced as it always did when she took the stage for the first time in any performance.

She visualized Garrett sitting all alone out there, smiling as she performed for him. She found her mark, looking off to the side, to Sabrina in the wings. She had her hands clutched together and was smiling wide. Kaylie took her position, smiled back, giving the thumbs up that she was ready.

The spotlight illuminated her and after a moment of applause the music started and once again Akaylia Michaels began to move.

The End

CPSIA information can be obtained
at www.ICGtesting.com
Printed in the USA
LVHW031037200322
713908LV00003B/472